Annie's War

Annie's War

By

Jacqueline Levering Sullivan

Eerdmans Books for Young Readers
Grand Rapids, Michigan / Cambridge, U.K.

Copyright © 2007 Jacqueline Levering Sullivan

Published 2007 by Eerdmans Books for Young Readers,
an imprint of Wm. B. Eerdmans Publishing Company

Wm. B. Eerdmans Publishing Company
2140 Oak Industrial Dr. NE, Grand Rapids, Michigan 49505
P.O. Box 163, Cambridge CB3 9PU U.K.

www.eerdmans.com/youngreaders

Manufactured in the United States of America

12 11 10 09   7 6 5 4 3 2

Library of Congress Cataloging-in-Publication Data

Sullivan, Jacqueline Levering.
Annie's war / written by Jacqueline Levering Sullivan.
p.   cm.
Summary: In 1946, imaginary conversations with President Truman help ten-year-old
Annie cope with having to live with her grandmother in Walla Walla, Washington, her
uncle's prejudice toward her grandmother's black tenant, and her intense desire for
news of her father, a pilot in the Army Air Corps who was reported missing in action.

ISBN 978-0-8028-5354-7(pbk: alk. paper)

[1. Family life — Washington — Fiction.   2. Grandmothers — Fiction.
3. Soldiers — Fiction.   4. Missing in action — Fiction.   5. Prejudices — Fiction.
6. African Americans — Fiction.   7. World War, 1939-1945 — Fiction.
8. Truman, Harry S., 1884-1972 — Fiction.
9. Washington (State) — History — 20th century — Fiction.]   I. Title.

PZ7.S9518Ann   2007
[Fic] — dc22

2007007067

Cover image by Bill Farnsworth
Text type set in Adobe Garamond

For Madeleine:

the finest in a long line of strong Howard women

Acknowledgments

I am deeply grateful to the friends and family who read this book in all its various stages, especially my writing group, Andra Simmons, Q. L. Pearce, Leah Key, Fran Rusackas, Mark Adam, and Gina Capaldi.

I am grateful to Betty Kovacs, a true and loving friend, who has read and listened to every word I have ever written. I also want to thank Doug Anderson, Mita Banerjee, and Carmen Fought for their constant support and encouragement.

Special thanks to Eerdmans, most particularly my editor, Shannon White, who loved Annie from the beginning and who instinctively knew how much more of her story I needed to tell.

Most of all I want to thank my husband, Jack, who

makes all things possible. And our children, Christopher, Gregory and Kevin.

Annie's story was inspired by memories of my grandmother, Hattie Howard, who taught by example the meaning of acceptance and tolerance.

A lazy July day at Grandma Hattie's Corner Grocery
in Walla Walla, Washington, circa 1940

Chapter 1

You wouldn't think a fellow as important as President Truman would leave the White House and travel clear across the country for a kid like me. But there he was, standing at the end of my hospital bed, dapper as could be in a fancy pinstripe suit. Just like in the newsreels at the picture show.

I blinked twice. He was still there. I had been lying there full of emptiness, feeling lonely and helpless as a newborn kitten. It wasn't clear to me right off just how Mr. Truman might be the answer to my prayers, but I was tickled pink he'd showed up.

"You look peaked, Annie Leigh," Mr. Truman said and took a large hanky out of his pocket and wiped his glasses. "You best mind the doctors now."

Darned if he didn't sit down at a big white piano and play a few notes.

"Needs a good piano tuner," he said, matter-of-factly. Then he flashed me that twinkly smile of his and played "The Missouri Waltz" clear through.

"That was real nice, sir." I wasn't sure what to call a president, and I couldn't get out of bed to curtsy. Did you curtsy for a president, or only for a queen?

"This must be important business, Annie Leigh," he said. "Why, you snatched me right out of a meeting with that bushy-browed Mr. Lewis. Nasty business, this coal strike. Makes me so mad I could spit tacks."

Mr. Lewis. That would be John L. Lewis. His old troll face had been scowling at me from the front page of *The News Tribune* for days. Bet Mr. Truman wasn't one bit sorry to hear from me.

"It's about my daddy," I said. "Do you know a Captain Eddie Howard? The Army Air Corps lost him. Being the president and all, I was sure you could find him."

Mr. Truman's eyes got all crinkly and he smiled. "Now that was downright careless. I can see you miss your daddy. Glad to help. I'll make finding him my first order of business when I get back to the White House."

"While you're at it, could you work on getting me out of this hospital?"

Mr. Truman looked me straight in the eye, all serious. He had on his about-to-make-a-speech face. "I'm afraid you're in the hospital for a spell," he said.

I tried to sit up. I wanted to have a serious conversation with him about Daddy, but clearly the president had important bills to sign or people to talk to because suddenly, without a word, he closed the piano lid and just got up and walked right through the wall. Then he was gone.

"Annie Leigh, open your eyes."

Now who was that? The voice sounded like Doctor Holly's, calling from about a hundred miles away. How was I supposed to answer him? And how did I get into this black tunnel, wrestling with the whirlies?

"Annie Leigh, it's Doctor Holly. Can you hear me? Can you open your eyes?"

There he was again. I figured he was talking through a bucket. His words made a big echo in my head. Then I heard another voice.

"Annie, baby, it's Mama. Open your eyes."

I was trying! I knew I had to get out of that tunnel but my eyelids were stuck, glued tight, and they wouldn't budge. I had just about given up hope of ever seeing daylight again when my eyes surprised me and flipped right open.

"Now then, there's my girl." Dr. Holly was looking down at me like a kindly grizzly bear. He smelled of Lifebuoy soap and Sir Walter Raleigh pipe tobacco.

"Do you know where you are, Annie Leigh?" he asked.

I tried to answer, but my mouth was full of flannel.

"Now don't move, Missy, you'll tear your stitches."

Didn't plan to move. But then the room took that very moment to buck like a bronco and a big ol' wave of sick came over me. Things happened pretty fast, and I had no other choice but to lean over the bed and puke all over Dr. Holly's shoes. Mama let out a yelp.

There I was, nearly eleven years old, and I couldn't keep my insides from slopping all over the floor. I hoped Mr. Truman wasn't anywhere around. It wouldn't do to throw up right in front of the president of these United States.

Dr. Holly was just as calm as could be, like it was the most natural thing in the world to have slimy vomit all over his shoes.

"Don't worry Mrs. Howard, that's the ether," he said to Mama. "But I'll need to check her bandages."

Dr. Holly leaned over me, and suddenly my right side felt like someone was ripping off a piece of tape in one fell swoop. I didn't know which was worse: throwing up all over or the ball of fire that had taken over my belly.

My appendix had busted open on the first of April. Some April Fool's. That morning they had rushed me to the hospital, I wondered if that appendix would pop right out of my skin like a plum pit or maybe burst open like a cherry bomb. But no! It just sat there making me feel sick as a dog. All the while everybody kept telling me, "Mind now, don't throw up."

Dr. Holly took a towel and wiped off his shoes and then fussed with my bandages as he talked to Mama.

"Now that's a fine looking incision," he said. "Annie Leigh's lucky. She'll just have a little scar on the right side. Seven inches or so. After all, we don't cut all the way across the belly like those ol' boys used to. Thought they were slicing open a melon." He patted my hand.

"A burst appendix is serious business, Annie Leigh. You'll be with us a while, but don't fret, you'll be right as rain by and by."

Well, I ended up spending the rest of that April and the first part of May in Saint Joseph's Hospital, eating a ton of mushy peas and watery custard and wishing I could be just about anywhere else. I should have known better than to wish for something real hard. The last thing I wanted to do was leave Mama alone for another summer without Daddy.

It had been a rough year. The very day we learned that President Roosevelt had died — April 12, 1945 — the telegram arrived telling us that Daddy was missing in action. Mr. Truman was right: that *was* downright careless! How had the Air Corps misplaced a fellow who stood six feet tall in his stocking feet and had hair the color of cinnamon?

I'd also spent the past year pretending not to hear Mama cry at night after she pulled the shades and shut her bedroom door. Why, sometimes she didn't even change out of her bathrobe the whole day.

Even though she insisted Daddy wasn't gone forever, Mama figured she'd already lost him. So when I just kept looking all puny and moped around the house with my chin practically on the floor, Doctor Holly suggested to Mama that maybe a change of scenery would do me good. I didn't much like leaving Mama alone, especially since she didn't seem to have one bit of happiness left in her. But I had to admit, I was real tired of being cooped up indoors playing checkers and watching my friends outside run ragged down the middle of Anderson Street.

I was hoping to see Mr. Truman again, but when I'd told Mama about him, she'd said he was just a figment of my imagination, with a little help from the ether. She said that Mr. Truman had enough to do running the country and getting everything back to normal after the war, and was hardly going to travel 3,000 miles for one busted appendix. And there most certainly was not a piano in my room at the hospital, she said. That was that.

"A few weeks with your Grandma Hattie will put the color back in your cheeks, and there's no reason in the world you can't go for a summer visit like always." Once Mama got a notion in her head, there was no changing it.

So the decision was made. Mama packed Daddy's old pigskin satchel, locked the doors up tight on our little yellow house in Seattle and drove me straight across the Cascades to Grandma Hattie's in Walla Walla.

That's how I came to be in Grandma's Corner Grocery the warm June day Miss Gloria Jean Washington came into our lives.

Chapter 2

Visits to Grandma's were usually like one long birthday party. I could always run into the store when I fancied a chocolate ice cream or a strawberry soda or a fistful of jelly beans. On slow mornings Grandma taught me swell things like how to make change or wrap a pound of ground round as smooth and fine as a Christmas package.

The Corner Grocery was a big square building attached to a Hansel and Gretel gingerbread house that had been cut up into three apartments. Grandma lived in the largest one on the first floor and rented out the two smaller ones upstairs. It was the "For Rent" sign that brought Miss Gloria into the store that particular morning.

On this day, like every other, Grandma was behind the counter by 8 a.m. counting the change into the till. She'd pop a peanut into her mouth and with the other hand roll the pennies and nickels out of their wrappers with one smooth snap of her wrists. My job was to take off the burlap that kept the vegetables fresh overnight. I was just folding the bags when someone knocked softly on the screen.

Grandma barely looked up. She was concentrating real hard on sorting the coins. Besides, no one ever knocked. The screen rattled, but still no one came in.

"Come in, come in, we're open," said Grandma, and she tucked the extra roll of nickels into the space in back of the coin tray and closed the drawer.

The screen door opened with a cheery tinkle and then a loud squawk. A soft voice said, "Excuse me, I've come about the apartment."

I looked up to find a tall colored lady standing near the door. I noticed her brown eyes first. They looked kind and sad all at the same time, but she smiled at me and her whole face just lit up. A gold lapel pin spelled out "Gloria" in perfect penmanship.

"Welcome, welcome." Grandma wiped her fingers on her apron and offered her hand. "I'm Hattie Howard and this is Miss Annie, my granddaughter. Do make yourself comfortable." Grandma was the only woman I knew who shook hands like a man.

"Pleased to meet you Ma'am." The lady then turned to me. "Nice to meet you, too, Miss Annie. I'm Miss Gloria." Her hand felt warm and soft inside my sweaty one.

"I have to warn you that the one apartment I have left is tiny," said Grandma. "Barely enough room for one. My son Billy is living in the larger one for now."

"I don't need much room, Ma'am." Miss Gloria took off her hat, a white straw with a bouquet of lilacs tumbling down the brim.

Her face glistened. She took a lavender handkerchief out of her pocket and dabbed at her forehead. The faintest whiff of violets floated in the air. I couldn't stop studying Miss Gloria's clothes. She was pretty as a picture. Her shoes were lavender to match the lilacs on her hat. Her suit was the same color with ribbons of purple along the lapels. She looked like Easter Sunday.

"Would you like to see the apartment then?" Grandma smoothed a few strands of hair back with the pencil she always kept tucked behind her ear.

"Oh, yes Ma'am," said Miss Gloria. She picked up her hat. "I'd like that very much."

"Please, call me Hattie." Grandma reached under the counter for a key. "What's your full name, dear?"

"It's Washington. Gloria Jean Washington." She gave me a big smile again.

"My full name is Annie Leigh Howard." I stood up straight and started to reach for her hand. The warm touch of her handshake was still working its way through me.

Grandma took just that moment to turn and motion Miss Gloria to follow her up the steps that led from the store into the hall outside the living room.

A few months earlier, Uncle Billy had cut a door right through the wall behind the candy counter. When he'd started as the butcher, he'd complained about how much trouble it was to get into the store from the main house. And his complaints hadn't stopped since! Daddy always said his little brother had a natural gift for building things, so I guess Billy was such a crosspatch cause he wanted to be working with wood instead of dead animals. But Grandma needed him in the store, and no one in town had much use for a grouchy carpenter.

The morning Miss Gloria came, Uncle Billy was grinding beef and fussing about something as usual. He'd gone to fight in the war at eighteen and returned home a year later all gloomy and cranky, acting like he knew everything. The old Billy was gone. No more silliness. No more practical jokes.

He'd shut his mouth pretty quick when Miss Gloria came in. In fact, he suddenly had important business inside the walk-in ice box. He stepped back out just in time to see Gloria following Grandma into the main house. He stood there like a ninny with his mouth open. I was just about to tell him he was going to swallow a fly when the phone rang.

Uncle Billy picked up the phone off the counter and turned his back on me. He seemed to be talking into a side of beef hanging inside the ice box. I couldn't make out what he was saying, but I could tell the words were coming out fast and furious. Seemed like the war had sucked any cheerfulness right out of Billy.

"Can you believe it? What's Ma thinking?" Billy hung up the phone and yanked off his apron. "Folks are calling already." He was out of the store in a flash. Mighty peculiar carrying on, even for Billy.

About ten minutes later Grandma and Miss Gloria came back down the steps together.

"It's all settled then," Grandma said. She walked over to the cold chest and took out three bottles of Orange Crush. The tops were off in a jiffy with the same smooth motion she used on the rolls of nickels.

"Nothing like an ice cold orange soda pop on a hot day like this one," said Grandma, taking a big old swallow. "And I'm afraid this summer is starting off a real scorcher."

"I'm used to weather hotter than this, Missus Howard. Why, in Georgia, where I'm from, this would feel like a spring morning." Miss Gloria's face broke out in the sweetest smile. "But this does hit the spot, and I thank you kindly for offering it."

Grandma drank orange soda pop on important occasions. I was so excited I gulped down my soda in three minutes flat, but Miss Gloria took only tiny little sips. I was still staring at her. Hadn't ever seen anyone with skin the color of caramel up close before. At first, when I saw her sad eyes, I thought she might be Mama's age, but when she smiled I could tell she wasn't much older than Uncle Billy.

I had lots of questions bubbling up inside. Like, how did she come to be in Walla Walla, all the way from Georgia? Seemed to me that must have been a real long trip.

The time I went to Texas with Mama and Daddy to visit his auntie, it was so far away we had to sleep two nights on the train. Bet a trip all the way from Georgia took at least three nights, maybe even four. Must be someone real special around here for Miss Gloria to come so far. Did she have a sweetheart out at the air base? I wondered.

I figured it wouldn't be polite to ask right off, so I kept quiet and watched the bottle of pop make wet spots grow on Miss Gloria's gloves. I started to ask her if she'd like a glass when Uncle Billy burst back in. He banged the screen door so hard the bell bounced right off the frame and dropped to the floor with a thunk.

Grandma let out a little gasp.

"For heaven's sakes, Billy. Whatever is the matter?"

Uncle Billy looked first at Grandma and then at Miss Gloria, and then he picked up the bell.

"Ma, could I talk to you?" Uncle Billy's face had broken out in red blotches, and beads of sweat were popping out on his forehead. He was all thumbs trying to reattach the bell.

"Are you ill, son?" The look on Grandma's face told me she was more annoyed than worried. She turned to Miss Gloria. "Excuse us."

She pointed to the back of the store and Uncle Billy lumbered off down the aisle with Grandma on his heels. It was just like Billy to be rude. Even though I hardly knew her, I wanted Miss Gloria to stay in the worst way. If Billy acted like a pill, she might just decide she couldn't stomach us Howards.

Before I could think what to say, the screen door flew open and that ornery Mrs. Hawkins from across the street waddled in. Just my luck. She usually came to pester Billy for free liver for her cats. He called her "Mrs. Hawkeyes" because she never missed a thing. If I goofed up on her change, she called me "young lady" in a voice that made me feel like a criminal. She had about ten cats, and rain or shine, she wore a raggedy old hat. And most peculiar, she was never without an apron, which she wore right on top of her suit.

"Good morning, Annabelle," said Mrs. Hawkins, in that snooty way she had. "Where are all the grownups this morning?" She was staring straight at Miss Gloria.

I was just about to remind her that my name wasn't Annabelle when Grandma walked up behind me.

"Now Evelyn, did you forget something? Billy forget to put the liver in your bag last night?"

"Well, Hattie, I . . . I need some soap powder. That's right, soap powder." Mrs. Hawkins held her pocket book like a shield in front of her and continued to stare straight ahead at Miss Gloria.

"My land," said Grandma, "I forgot my manners. Evelyn, this is Gloria Jean Washington. She's just rented the front apartment upstairs."

"Pleased to meet you, Ma'am," said Miss Gloria, smiling one of her sweet smiles.

Mrs. Hawkins didn't say a word. She made a funny gurgling sound in her throat and started for the door. She was mumbling to herself, but I caught her meaning plain as day. Expect everyone else did as well. That old busybody was going on about Grandma taking in outsiders, and what was she thinking, and something about "not our kind of folks."

Well, that Mrs. Hawkins had another think coming if she thought my grandma would abide ugly talk like that. Honestly, what kind of welcome was that for someone as nice as Miss Gloria? That old busybody rushed out the door so fast she forgot her soap powder. Nobody moved to go after her.

Everything just turned still for a moment. No one

made a sound. Then Grandma shook her head, gave Miss Gloria her key, and Gloria started up to her new apartment.

As soon as she was upstairs, Uncle Billy cornered Grandma. I heard his voice rise to a pitiful whine. I hoped we didn't have to listen to him complain the whole darn day.

A few minutes later, the screen door swung open and the first of a steady stream of customers entered the store, so I had to get busy. Good thing, too, 'cause I was getting madder by the minute. Billy was just too big for his britches. He needed a trip to the woodshed or his mouth washed out with soap. I wasn't sure I could manage either one of those, but the next time Billy opened his big mouth he just might find my fist in it.

Chapter 3

We didn't see much of Miss Gloria for a few days. Once in a while I could hear her moving around upstairs, and the smell of her violet perfume told me when she'd gone through the back hall. Mostly, she stayed to herself in the apartment that had once been Daddy's bedroom and the sun porch.

On the morning of the Fourth of July, Grandma sent me to ask Miss Gloria to our picnic. She seemed real happy to be asked. I explained to her that every year the whole neighborhood gathered in the cool grassy area near where the creek ran through our backyard. Grandma supplied the sodas and frankfurters and her famous potato salad, and everyone else brought heaps of coleslaw and beans and lemon sponge cakes. Uncle Billy cranked out gallons of homemade strawberry ice cream. Everyone ate 'til they nearly burst, and then we walked down to the schoolyard to hear the band and watch the fireworks.

"I know just what I'll make," said Miss Gloria, and she looked real pleased with herself. "Now scoot, I need to get started."

About 2:30 in the afternoon, we were just putting extra sodas in the cold box when Grandma checked her lapel watch, which was pinned to the collar of her Sunday dress.

"My land, where is everybody?" she said.

Usually people began to gather before 2:00, eager for the chance to gossip and let their kids run wild. Even Uncle Billy was missing. I followed Grandma out to the yard where three long tables waited, their white butcher paper tablecloths rattling in the light breeze.

"Grandma, Billy hasn't even started the ice cream," I said. Leave it to Billy to spoil the day without even half trying. "What's holding everybody up? I told Miss Gloria there'd be tons of neighbors here."

Grandma took another look at her watch and tugged at her ear. Hard. She had a way of doing that when she was all out of sorts. "Who says a picnic requires dozens of people?" she said. "Good food and a few hungry folks are all we need."

Miss Gloria came out of the house carrying a large dish. The smell made my stomach rumble.

"Oh, boy! Peach cobbler!"

"It's *Georgia* peach cobbler." Miss Gloria smiled and waved it past my nose. "Well, I'm not sure about the peaches, but the recipe is certainly from Georgia," she said, setting down the dish at the end of one of the tables.

Just as she turned around, I saw someone dart behind the garage. Then something whizzed past my ear and hit Grandma's silver coffee urn with a loud kerplunk.

"Now what in tarnation was that?" Grandma rushed to steady the urn teetering on the edge of the card table and then turned her attention to Miss Gloria. "Are you all right, dear? That thing sailed so close to you! Why, you might have been hurt!"

That thing turned out to be a good sized rock. My stomach did a flip. Was someone throwing rocks at Grandma? Or maybe even at Miss Gloria? This afternoon wasn't turning out at all like it was supposed to. I didn't understand what was going on, but I was about mad enough to spit tacks! By now all the tables should have been piled high with food, and there wasn't a sponge cake or a jellyroll in sight. Not to mention I had my heart set on sampling four kinds of pie. Miss Gloria was going to think I was a big fibber.

Grandma didn't say too much, but I could tell she was upset, too. It was now almost 3:00 and Billy was still nowhere in sight. And the only neighbors who had shown up were old Mr. Teeples from Grandma's Bible study and Opal Bailey, who was deaf as a post, always had a cheek full of tobacco, and could out-cuss any farmhand for miles around. Usually not the kind of folks who made someone mad enough to pitch rocks. I didn't want Miss Gloria to think Walla Walla was full of rowdies, so I figured I'd just go down by the garage and have myself a look.

I'd been hoping all morning that Mr. Truman would show up. I bet he'd figure it would be worth the trip for some of Grandma's potato salad. And he would have been real welcome. Anyone thinking of throwing rocks with Harry S. Truman around had another think coming.

"Annie, stop dawdling," Grandma said. "That ice cream isn't going to freeze itself."

I didn't want to upset Grandma, so my search would have to wait. Grandma was getting a little crabby because her picnic wasn't coming together like she planned. Miss Gloria and I went to work on the ice cream, and she had just taken a turn at the crank when Billy finally showed up.

"Where've you been, mister?" I stood up to my full four-feet five-inches and used my best grown-up voice. "You're in *big* trouble."

"Be quiet, twerp." Uncle Billy turned and coughed up an ugly gob of spit that landed a short distance from where Miss Gloria had just been standing.

"You're the big twerp," I said. "Ick! You just about spit in the ice cream."

Billy put his face right in front of mine and rolled his eyes. He smelled like he'd taken a bath in a tub of whiskey. I almost passed out. Grandma was going to have a fit. She was against spirits of any kind. He'd done dumb things before, but Billy had never come home smelling of liquor. Before I could go tattle on him, a voice called out from the shadows near the garage.

"Hey, Missus Howard, you takin' up with colored folks now?"

I felt my face burn. I looked at Miss Gloria. She was concentrating real hard on the crank. Grandma held onto the silver spoon she had in her hand and moved over to stand next to Miss Gloria.

"Missus Howard, I asked you a question." The shadowy figure stumbled into the yard.

Grandma held her ground, but her face was beet red. "Ben Jackson, I'll thank you kindly to leave at once."

No one moved. Sober, Ben Jackson was plain ornery, but a little whiskey made him a hundred times uglier. By this time I had moved even closer to Gloria. I grabbed her hand. It was ice cold.

"And Orville," said Grandma, turning to Mr. Teeples, "please pour Billy a cup of that good coffee."

Uncle Billy looked a little green, but he didn't refuse the coffee. A few minutes later he ran behind the tool shed, and we all pretended we couldn't hear him puke his guts out into the creek. About that time Ben Jackson disappeared behind the garage, rambling on about some foolishness.

"Don't pay him no mind, Hattie," Opal Bailey yelled into Grandma's ear. And if she didn't turn around and spit a big wad of tobacco in the direction of the garage! For once, Grandma acted like she didn't even mind.

After all that, no one had much of an appetite. I even

turned down a third helping of Grandma's potato salad. I noticed Miss Gloria was just sitting there pushing hers around on her plate. By and by, I dished up bowls of peach cobbler and Grandma topped them off with a big spoonful of strawberry ice cream. Didn't seem right to let that Georgia peach cobbler go to waste.

"How do you get that biscuit crust so fluffy, Gloria?" said Grandma, trying hard to make the best of things.

Even after Miss Bailey and Mr. Teeples joined in and couldn't say enough about that scrumptious cobbler, I knew the perfect day I'd promised Miss Gloria was ruined. Funny thing was, last year we'd welcomed Billy home with the biggest Fourth of July picnic I'd ever seen. Practically the whole town had shown up. Now I was so mad at Billy, I could've punched him in the nose. I would have, too, except there was a roller coaster having a fine time in my stomach. So I just sat there and watched while Grandma pretended that her picnic had worked out just swell.

For the next few days, I was pretty bored. I wrote a letter to Mama, like I did every week, but I didn't have much to say to her. Didn't want to let on about Billy's nasty ol' self. But Grandma and Gloria were chatting constantly, and I knew they had their heads together about something.

On Sunday, Grandma invited Gloria to have dinner with us. Billy looked real glum the whole meal, but he didn't say a word. When Grandma announced over the berry pie that she'd hired Gloria to help her with the book-keeping, Billy came close to choking on a mouthful. I wanted to reach under the table and give him a good pinch, but out of respect for Miss Gloria I behaved myself.

"I'll go get the Orange Crush," I said and bolted down the hall into the store.

When I got back to the kitchen, Billy was gone, and Grandma and Miss Gloria were bent over an old ledger. None of us sitting around the table that night had any idea that Uncle Billy's days at Grandma's were numbered. And no one could have predicted that Gloria and I would both be there long after he'd left. It's true that Billy had become a sour apple. But until Gloria Jean Washington came to Walla Walla, no one suspected he was also downright mean.

Chapter 4

After Billy and his new pal Ben Jackson had acted like such fools at the picnic, Billy had started staying out 'til all hours. When he showed up late at the store, morning after morning, he would sass Grandma and cuss in front of the customers. I figured cussing was just another thing the army taught Billy. Why, before he went away to war, I never even heard him say "Heck." Grandma liked to tell the story about the time Billy smashed his finger in the door of the preacher's car. He started jumping around yelling, "Holy Rollers! Holy Rollers!" until Grandma popped his hand into an ice-cold pitcher of lemonade. I would have bet my allowance that Billy was smart enough to watch his step around Grandma after he came home drunk on the Fourth. I was wrong.

One late afternoon, just at closing time, Miss Gloria came into the store to count the cash and get the day's charge slips. She was laying out the five- and one-dollar bills. She always stacked them neatly into bundles before she did the day's receipts.

Uncle Billy was next to her at the register in two long strides. He grabbed her wrist and put his face real close to hers. "Listen here, I'm watching you every minute."

Billy's grip tightened and Miss Gloria's arm began to wrinkle from the pressure. I figured he was going to break her wrist.

"You even think of snitching some of that money," he said, "and you'll wish you were back pickin' cotton."

I wanted to sink into the floorboards. What had gotten into Billy? He was acting like some evil genie had popped out of a cod liver oil bottle and was spreading all his oily nastiness around. I tried to say something, but when I opened my mouth nothing came out.

Neither Billy nor I knew how long Grandma had been standing just inside the door, but she'd heard and seen enough.

"Now just which money might that be, son?" she asked.

Billy let go of Miss Gloria's arm real fast and jumped back like he'd just dodged a bullet. Grandma was furious! I was hoping she'd slap him silly, but she didn't. I bet later he wished she had. Grandma started to say something, but stopped. Her mouth turned into a solid straight line before she spoke.

"William Matthew Howard, I believe you owe Miss Washington an apology." Grandma's words came out hard through clenched teeth.

William Matthew Howard. Billy's full Christian name. That meant trouble.

Uncle Billy mumbled something. All this time Miss Gloria had been quiet as a mouse. She just stood next to the counter rubbing her arm.

"I didn't hear that, William." The starch in Grandma's voice said she meant business. Uncle Billy's goose was cooked.

Instead of an apology, Billy threw down his butcher's apron and turned to Grandma. His face was all red and shiny.

"I'll quit before I'll apologize to darkie trash."

The look on Grandma's face told him he'd gone too far. I thought any minute she'd spit fire.

"Billy, you are no better than Ben Jackson." Grandma had gone to stand by the door. "Leave this instant and don't come back."

She held open the screen. "You can return tomorrow for your things."

Uncle Billy shuffled his feet, trying to buy some time, but Grandma didn't budge. Finally, Billy marched out the screen door, slamming it just hard enough to make his point. The bell gave a half-hearted tinkle and then fell smack on the floor. I made a move to pick it up, but Grandma raised her hand.

"Leave it, child," she said. "I never liked the sound of the dang thing anyway."

Throwing Uncle Billy out took a terrible toll on Grandma. She didn't mope around, but she got real quiet. It was bad enough that the army had lost Daddy. Grandma had a special spot in her heart for him — she always said he could charm roses off wallpaper. But, now, having Billy turn into a mean no-account — that was the last straw. Grandma was in the store every morning, just like usual, but she didn't exchange small talk with the customers or kid around with the mailman.

One night a week or so later, Billy finally came for a few clothes. Grandma stayed in her room the whole time he was in the house. He left without saying a word to anyone, not even a "Hey, twerp" to me. Miss Gloria came down a little later to work on the books, and when she saw we hadn't eaten, she poked around in the kitchen and began to fix dinner. The smell of cornbread baking soon filled the house. I brought the sun tea in from the back steps and sat down to snap some beans.

Miss Gloria was just putting the final touches on a potato casserole when Grandma appeared in the kitchen.

"Good heavens, Gloria," she said. "You must have read my mind." Grandma sat down next to me and grabbed a handful of the beans. "I was having a little lie-down, just wishing dinner could fix itself."

"This poor child looked about to starve," said Miss Gloria, and she gave me a wink. "Couldn't stand by and let a ten-year-old child go without her supper now, could I?"

No one said a word about Billy over dinner, but he was there all right, like some nasty old ghost. I wanted to tell Miss Gloria how sorry I was and what a big dumb cluck

Billy was, but I kept my mouth shut. I didn't want to upset Grandma by bringing the whole ugly business up again. Besides, ten hundred apologies weren't going to make up for Billy's words. "Darkie trash." I didn't quite know what that meant, but I knew it was downright nasty. I wouldn't have been one bit surprised if a slimy old toad hopped right out of his mouth after that. I got chills just thinking about it.

Before the week was out, Mr. Teeples' nephew Scooter came to replace Billy as the butcher. Grandma bustled around the store as always, but her forehead had a permanent wrinkle in it. She was down in the dumps, and I wanted my old Grandma back. I knew she was probably still tied in knots over the whole mess, and I decided I needed to help her.

I'd been making real serious plans to write the Army Air Corps and tell them to find my daddy, but I decided that talking to Uncle Billy was more important. I had to get him to apologize for being such a fool. I sure didn't miss the bratty old things he did, like the time he put a mouse down my pajamas, but he was acting a thousand times worse than that. When I tracked him down, I was going to ask him what happened to the silly old uncle I used to have. I'd let him know what a sorry excuse he was for a human being and that he'd just about killed Grandma. She'd always treated folks kindly and taught us to do the same.

Billy hadn't been himself since he'd come back from the war, but he really had a burr in his tail after Miss Gloria came. I'd never seen him act so rotten around new folks before, and I decided to find out why.

First, I needed to have a long talk with Mr. Truman. He knew a thing or two about wars, so I figured he'd know what to do about Billy. I sure hoped he'd bring his piano.

Chapter 5

I stood at the window and watched the streetlights go on down Third Street. Some nights it seemed like the dark started at one end of the city and slowly spread out around the houses and fences and alleys like warm molasses. Other times it just plopped straight down in one fell swoop like a big pot of ink had spilled from the sky. I liked to think Daddy was somewhere in the world looking up into the night sky and wishing he was sitting out on the back steps with me naming the stars. His absence sat heavy in my heart.

"C'mon, Sweetpea. Let's wrestle that Murphy bed down." Grandma was standing in the doorway that led to the kitchen. Her hair was hanging in long strands and her face looked tired and full of sorrow. Uncle Billy was most likely sitting heavy in Grandma's heart.

As for that old bed, how I hated to have to fool with it! I worried one of these days it just might take a notion to swing up and pop right back into the wall with me in it. I wouldn't have turned down a night on the lumpy living room sofa.

After Grandma had tucked me in and heard my prayers, I asked her if she thought Mr. Truman could find me in Walla Walla.

"He's a busy man," said Grandma. "I wouldn't be disappointed if he doesn't track you down, Annie Leigh." She smoothed the covers and gave me a big sloppy kiss. And if I wasn't mistaken, she gave me a wink as well.

A dozen questions were making themselves at home in my head, and I wasn't going to sleep until I'd sorted out some answers. My eyes kept trying to close, but I told myself I had to concentrate real hard on what to do about Billy. Though he made me so mad I could spit tacks, I was absolutely not going to give up on him. Daddy would expect nothing less from me.

I was so tired I needed toothpicks to prop my eyes open, but Mr. Truman snapped me to attention. There he was, big as you please, sitting in Grandma's rocker in a fancy white suit, holding a fancy straw hat in one hand and a walking stick in the other.

"I'm mighty glad to see you, sir. I was afraid you might not find me in Walla Walla," I said.

"Very little gets past me. I was out for my evening stroll and suddenly had the most powerful need to visit some of Walla Walla's fine orchards. Being stuck in the White House, sometimes I do miss farm country." The president leaned forward and wrapped his hands around his walking stick. "It's been a while, Annie Leigh."

"You want me to run into the store and get you an apple? Grandma eats one every single day. I think it's practically the law in Walla Walla." I could hear myself rambling. The president was going to think I was a dodo bird. "I like apples best in pies or dipped in caramel," I added.

"Something you want to talk about, Annie Leigh?" Mr. Truman sat up straight with a somber look on his face. It was the same expression he wore in newsreels when he was talking to General Eisenhower or giving orders to his cabinet.

"Yes sir. I still really want you to find my daddy, but right now I need to have a talk about my Uncle Billy. He's just been an awful pill since he came back from the war. And since Gloria came he's been downright ugly. Can't figure out why. Because she's different, maybe? Not from around here? Or do you think it's because she's colored? That would be an awful dumb reason. Why, when she's around, I can't help keeping a smile on my face all day long." I had to stop for a little gasp of air. "And, another thing, Billy's hanging out with bad folks." I whispered the last part. "And he's drinking whiskey."

Mr. Truman seemed to think all of that over for a second.

"War does terrible things to a man, Annie Leigh," he said finally. "Down in the trenches, you have to put yourself in a place where nothing can touch you. Talk to him straight. You should tell your uncle how you feel. I bet he'd listen to you."

"That's what I was thinking. But Billy's a stubborn cuss."

Mr. Truman let out a little chuckle. "Now stubborn, that's a condition I know a thing or two about." Thunder rumbled and roared outside. The president stood up and put on his hat.

"Sounds like a summer storm is coming. I best be

getting back. The secret service is going to wonder where in the world I've got to and Bess will have a fit if I get this new suit wet."

Then he gave me one of those fine smiles of his and disappeared right out the front door without bothering to open it. That was a neat trick of his. One of these days I'd have to ask him how he did it. And another thing I wanted to know: what did that S stand for in Harry S. Truman?

Talking to Billy I could do. Finding Billy was going to be the hard part. I knew where to run errands for Grandma and how to find my way to the pictures and back, but that's about all I knew about Walla Walla. I didn't have the slightest idea where Billy had gone. Everyone knew that Ben Jackson hung around Halverson's Feed and Fuel, but I wasn't about to track him down. First off, Grandma wouldn't like me going off by myself. And I couldn't very well ask Miss Gloria to help me. So I decided I was going to have to do a little detective work on my own. Since Scooter was Billy's age, I thought I'd start with him.

I got my chance a few days later. Grandma left for a Chamber of Commerce meeting downtown and put

Scooter in charge of the store. I walked her to the bus and then ran back home as fast as I could.

Scooter was arranging lamb chops in the meat case like they were precious jewels. He had little rows of parsley lining the trays and tiny ruffled paper hats on the end of the chops. Seemed to me he was going to a whole lot of trouble for a bunch of raw meat. I grabbed an icy root beer out of the cold case and went over to see what I could find out.

"Pretty early in the morning for a soda pop, ain't it?" said Scooter.

"Grandma lets me have pop for breakfast all the time," I lied.

Scooter just smiled and shook his head. While I watched, he piled freshly ground beef onto a clean tray and molded it into a fat oblong. I hadn't come to make small talk with Scooter, so I thought I'd get right to it.

"You ever see my uncle around?" I asked.

"Naw." Scooter had moved on to bacon, and was laying out slices in perfect parallel rows. "Billy doesn't have much time for his old pals these days." He shrugged. "I hear he's running with a pretty tough bunch."

"I don't know what's gotten into Uncle Billy. He's got Grandma all upset, and he was real nasty to Miss Gloria.

When I find him, I'm going to give him a piece of my mind."

"I heard about what happened from Uncle Orville," Scooter said, wiping his hands on his apron. He leaned against the end of the counter. "A kid like you shouldn't mess with those rough boys, though. I'll check around and see what I can find out."

Before I could tell him I was turning eleven at the end of the summer, and nearly grown, the door swung open and a bunch of giggling neighbor ladies came in. Scooter gave me a little wave and shuffled back to the other side of the counter to wait on them.

I could hear Miss Gloria singing out by the clothesline, so I went to see what she was up to. I was still trying to find the right words to tell her how sorry I was about Uncle Billy acting so hateful, but they just wouldn't come.

"Land sakes, it's hot this morning!" said Miss Gloria. She handed me the end of a sheet. "Child, help me hang this so it doesn't drop to the ground."

We hung the rest of the clothes, and then I turned the crank while she put the next load through the wringer. Mama never let me help with laundry at home. She was always afraid I'd wring out my arm instead of a pillowcase.

"I made some biscuits this morning," said Gloria after we'd finished. "Wait here, and I'll bring you a couple."

I pulled two of the old lawn chairs closer to the creek where it was cooler and brought over a milk crate for a table. Miss Gloria was back in a jiffy carrying a tray with two glasses of lemonade and a plate of golden biscuits with jam.

"Now this is nice," she said.

Miss Gloria set the tray on the crate and pulled a chair closer to mine. "I can feel just the tiniest breeze coming off the water." She lay back against the headrest and closed her eyes. "Do you ever listen to the music it makes at night?" she asked.

"I guess I never really thought about it." The creek had always been there, but I'd never really listened to it. Now, I had noticed the music of Miss Gloria's voice. It had a kind of rhythm to it, the way her words stretched out like the verses in a hymn, with a hint of sadness.

"I'm real glad you came here, Miss Gloria," I said. "Are you glad you're here?"

Miss Gloria handed me a glass of lemonade before she answered. "I'm glad I found you and your grandmother, but life has a way of turning out different from the way we planned."

The sunlight caught a tear on Miss Gloria's cheek so small I might have missed it. She continued. "But I want you to know that being here with you and your grandma has brought me real comfort."

Now I felt really bad. Uncle Billy hadn't been much comfort. He'd been a spiteful mean soul.

"Miss Gloria," I started to say. The words caught in my throat. I looked at the ground, trying to get the words unstuck. "I've been trying to think how to make it up to you. That is, for Uncle Billy being so mean and ugly. I don't know what's got into him."

I sat for a minute trying to think what to say next.

"And now I've made you cry."

Miss Gloria came over and knelt down next to my chair. She took my hand and patted it softly.

"Sweet thing, you didn't make me cry." She stood up. "Come on, let's go put our feet in the creek and cool off. Then I'll tell you a story."

Just the way she said it, I knew it had to be important.

Chapter 6

I took off my ugly old oxfords in a flash and stuffed my socks into the toes. I hated those stiff old boards! I eased my toes into the cold creek water and wiggled them around.

For the rest of the morning Miss Gloria and I sat on the bank with our feet dangling in the cold water. The day was hot as blazes, and I was tempted to just jump in. When I was little, the neighborhood kids and I had tried to launch leaf rafts and paper boats. But after I slipped and broke my wrist one summer, I thought twice about playing in the water. I knew, sure as shootin', that old creek would get me.

I splashed my feet around a little and waited for Miss Gloria to tell her story. She hadn't said a word since we took off our shoes. I was thinking that after I'd heard her story, I could tell Miss Gloria about my daddy. I bet she'd be surprised to hear that the Army had up and lost him.

After a while Miss Gloria reached over and snapped a few blossoms off Grandma's hollyhock bushes. "You ever make a hollyhock doll, Annie?"

"I never played with dolls much." Shoot! Didn't seem like Miss Gloria was ever going to get to her story.

"See, you use the blossom for the skirt, and then very carefully, you make a hole in the stem end and poke in a bud for the head."

Not ten minutes later, Miss Gloria had a whole wedding party of pink-and-white blossom dolls lined up next to the creek. She started singing, silly like, and dancing those dolls around. Then Miss Gloria started talking in a teeny weeny voice, like it was the dolls talking. I couldn't help myself, I started laughing. I never had seen an adult person act sillier than a kid! Miss Gloria started giggling too, and pretty soon we were splashing water on each other. We were laughing and carrying on so that we didn't hear Uncle Billy come around the corner.

"Annie Leigh, you best get your butt over here now." He was standing near the screen door that went into the back porch. His face was so scrunched up into a big ol' frown, I'd swear he was wearing a devil mask.

"Wait 'til I tell Grandma you said a bad word," I yelled back at him. I'd been trying to wish Billy back home to make amends, but now that he was here, I wished I hadn't wasted my time. "You can't boss me around, Mister," I said. "Besides, where you been? You're in big trouble." My shoes were still over by the creek. I picked them up and took my time putting them back on.

Some ugly critter had taken hold of Billy. He wasn't happy unless he could stir up some kind of hornet's nest and make a mess of trouble for somebody. Grandma said he still had the war rattling around in his head. She said that killing folks was just not natural. That for a fellow to shoot someone dead in wartime, he'd have to turn off any goodness he had in his heart. Grandma figured Billy would come around after he got used to being home, but I thought his heart was still as cold as one of the creek stones.

"You heard me, Missy! You get in the house right now." Uncle Billy was trying hard to look fierce, but he just looked silly with his skinny old arms crossed over his puny chest.

"Miss Gloria and I are having a tea party," I said. "Boys aren't invited. Besides, she was just getting ready to tell me a story."

"You can't stay out here with her." Billy tipped his head in Miss Gloria's direction and scowled.

"This is a free country. I can stay out here if I like, Mr. Bossy Billy."

Uncle Billy moved so fast, I didn't have time to get out of his way. He grabbed me by one arm and gave me a good whack across the face. I let out a yelp and then ran back to Miss Gloria. I was working real hard not to cry. I was going to show Uncle Billy it took more than a slap to make me blubber.

"You had no call to strike this child, Mr. Howard," Miss Gloria said. She pulled me closer to her. "Look at that mark on her face. What's Missus Howard going to say?"

"You leave my mama out of this." Uncle Billy looked like he wanted to grab Miss Gloria, but his hands were shaking so bad, he jammed them into his pockets instead. "None of your business no how."

Billy scraped at the ground with the heel of his shoe. "Caused nothing but trouble ever since you got here."

Miss Gloria hugged me tighter, but I wriggled free and marched right over to Billy.

"You're the meanest person in the whole world, Billy Howard." I was too mad to be afraid. "I hate you! I hope you eat worms and die!" Then I kicked him a good one right in the shins. For the first time ever, I was happy to be wearing those old oxfords.

"What the —" Billy reached down and grabbed his leg. "Why, you little . . . !" He was for sure about to take another whack at me, but Miss Gloria stepped between us.

"Mr. Howard, I'm going to take this child into the house now and get her some ice," she said. "Looks like a bruise is beginning to blossom." Miss Gloria put her hand on my shoulder and moved me toward the house. "I'm sure Annie's sorry she kicked you. Aren't you, Annie?"

"No I'm not. Not one bit." I tried to break free from Miss Gloria, but by now she had a firm grip on my shoulders. Billy was too busy rubbing his shin to come after us. I bet either one of us could have knocked him over with a feather. He hadn't expected this turn of events.

Back in the kitchen, Miss Gloria pounded ice cubes into little pieces, while I kept running my fingers over my cheek, checking for any sign of a bump.

"Billy had that kick coming," I said. "Truly, I'm not the least bit sorry."

"That might be so," said Miss Gloria, "but you don't want his meanness to rub off on you. Then you become no better than he is." She took a handful of ice chips and wrapped them in a washcloth. "Here, put this on your cheek. We don't want your grandmother to see you with a big welt on your face."

"Well, still, I'm not sorry. Because of him, I didn't get to hear your story. I'd like to punch Uncle Billy a good one right in his snout!"

"Hush child," said Miss Gloria, "You're real angry now. I am, too. There's no excuse for your uncle's behavior, but you can't let that anger boil over inside. It's better to keep it at a slow simmer until it just evaporates. Then before you know it, you've let it all go." She took a breath, then let it out slowly. "Growing up where I did, you learned real fast that staying mad gets you nothing but a bellyache. Now, your Uncle Billy, why, he's holding in so much meanness, it's just rusting out his belly."

"Maybe he'll shrivel up and die," I said.

"A person with that much poison inside, he's already

dead." Miss Gloria checked the washcloth and added more ice.

"Uncle Billy was always a rascal, but since he came back from the war he's acted awful peculiar. Even when I was a terrible pest, Billy never hit me before."

"Sad thing is," said Miss Gloria, "young men go to war and they come back bitter old men." She reached for the soggy washcloth and patted my cheek dry with the corner of a tea towel. "That is, if they come back at all."

Miss Gloria started swallowing real hard, so I stayed quiet and didn't mention another word about not hearing her story. I wasn't real sure what all she was saying, but one thing I did know: getting mad at Uncle Billy had put little hammers in my head and made my stomach churn. Maybe the rust had already started.

Chapter 7

When noon rolled around and still no Grandma, I begged four slices of bologna off Scooter and made Miss Gloria and me sandwiches for lunch. I put extra mayo on Miss Gloria's and added a slice of cheese. It was after one o'clock before Grandma finally got home. Miss Gloria and I were sitting out on the back steps talking and picking at the last of the crumbs.

Grandma looked all done in. Her straw hat had wilted so the shiny red cherries drooped over one ear. Gloria jumped up and went to get her one of the lawn chairs. Grandma sat down and put her worn leather satchel next to her on the ground. Mama always said Grandma should carry a proper pocketbook, that respectable business-women didn't carry scuffed satchels that looked like old shoes. I thought her satchel looked mysterious, like those bags spies carried in the picture shows.

"Those men from city hall do go on," said Grandma. "I don't know how they ever . . ." She stopped mid-sentence. "What happened to your face, Annie?"

My words came out in a rush. "Uncle Billy slapped me real hard, and he used a bad word, and he tried to make Miss Gloria leave, and . . ." I ran out of breath and stopped.

"Billy was here?" said Grandma. She took off her hat. I couldn't help but notice her fingers trembled when she tugged at the hat pins. She sat forward in her chair, and I figured she was going to ask about Billy. Instead, she reached out her hand. "Come over here, Sweetpea, and let me look at you."

I walked over to her, knowing once she got a good look at my face, Billy was going to be in a heap more trouble. Most days, I could hardly wait to tattle on him, but this time I felt different. She'd had enough aggravation.

Grandma took my face in her hands. "That's a mighty ugly bruise, Annie Leigh." She took in a big breath of air and let it out real slow. Miss Gloria sat there nodding like she agreed.

For what seemed like ages, the air was real still. The only sound came from the creek, where even the water was making soft whispery sounds. Grandma stood up and put her hands on her hips. That was her "thinking it over" position. When she was upset, she hardly ever yelled or stomped her foot like Mama. She just got real quiet. I was pretty sure she carried the hurt around with her and let it gnaw on her for a bit. Whenever she got that way, I almost wished she'd holler and carry on.

"Annie, why don't you go treat yourself to a cold soda pop. Your old Grandma needs to talk to Gloria for a bit."

Two sodas in one day were usually a big treat, but even on that hot day I didn't feel like one. When I got to the store, it was empty except for Scooter. Business had been slow. Mostly just the old regulars came in, and then they barely bought anything, maybe a wedge of cheese or a RC cola. We hadn't even seen Mrs. Hawkins since the day Gloria came.

Scooter was scrubbing off the meat counter. The whole store smelled like bleach. I went over and sat in a corner by the potato bin and sipped a strawberry soda. No use letting Scooter get a good look at my face. That would only give the neighbors something more to jaw on.

❖   ❖   ❖

Since Billy left, Gloria had been eating with us most nights. She and Grandma took turns doing the cooking, and I helped with the washing up. But that night Grandma and I had dinner all by ourselves.

Grandma had made upside-down lemon sponge custard for dessert, my favorite. She let me have a big helping, too. I did everything but lick the bowl clean like a cat. She cleared her throat a couple of times, and I knew we were going to have what she called a "heart-to-heart."

I didn't look up, but kept my eyes on the last few bits of pudding. The last time Grandma had done so much throat clearing, we'd had a heart-to-heart about me leaving my skates in the hall. She had taken a tumble and banged her knee real good. This time I was sure she'd decided to send me home early so she could get down to straightening Billy out. Boy, I was way wrong about that.

"Annie," said Grandma. "How would you like to stay with your old Granny for a while longer, maybe even through the school year?" She had that funny happy sound to her voice grownups always get when they want you to think a bad idea is a really good one.

"That's a real swell idea, especially with Gloria here and all." I stopped to take a deep breath. "But I should go home just before Labor Day like we planned. I miss Mama, and Daddy will be home any day now. President Truman will find him. I know he will."

Grandma studied a spot on the ceiling before she reached across the table for my hands. "You do understand, Annie, that the war has been over nearly a year now?"

"You wait and see. Daddy's not dead!" I said. I needed to stop and take another big breath. "He just isn't."

"Oh, child." Grandma's shoulders drooped and her mouth started moving, but no words came out, just a deep sigh. She studied something out the window for a while before she continued. "Your mama and I both thought you might like to stay with me for a bit longer."

"You talked to Mama? How come she didn't ask to talk to me? And another thing, I've written her four letters, and she hasn't answered one!" I couldn't look at Grandma. "Doesn't Mama want me to come home?"

"Now, Annie, it's nothing like that. Your mama loves you a lot." Grandma reached across the table and touched my cheek. "Look at me, child." She took a small tin of salve out of her pocket and gently touched my cheek with small dabs.

"Your mama's got a lot on her mind. She has a new job, and she's thinking about moving into a new place. She needs time to settle herself in." Grandma put more sugar in her voice. "We'll give her a call when she gets her new phone. But, for now, why don't you write her another letter? You can even use my special blue stationery with the forget-me-nots on the border."

No fancy blue paper was going to make up for not talking to Mama. It wasn't going to fix that chunk of something hard wedged in right next to my heart, either. Only hearing Mama, in her very own voice, say that she loved me and was missing me a whole bunch could do that.

"Mama's been by herself for most of a month," I said. "She made such a fuss about me coming here, and now she doesn't want me to come home."

"Annie, you know better than that." Grandma shook her head. "Now I don't want to hear any more of that silly talk."

Bet Grandma didn't know about that dentist, the stork, the one whose legs stuck out right from under his arms. Now that I thought about it, he hung around a lot. He'd started sniffing around Mama right after I got out of the hospital. Played like he was checking up on me. Even I knew dentists don't make house calls.

That made me so mad I thought maybe I would just stay in Walla Walla and not go back home for a million, trillion years. I'd tell the army to send Daddy back to Grandma's. If the army had to go and lose somebody, how come they lost Daddy and not Uncle Billy? And why did Uncle Billy come home from Italy with his head so full of meanness and war that he couldn't fit in anything else? It was hard to figure grownups out sometimes.

I hoped Harry S. Truman didn't have any important bills to sign or letters to write, because I most certainly had a million more important things to talk over with him, and there wasn't a minute to lose.

Chapter 8

"And I don't want to sleep in this Murphy bed one more night, let alone for the whole school year! Some morning Grandma's going to find nothing but little bitty parts of my fingers poking out from where the bed frame's stuck in the wall."

Mr. Truman was sitting in his usual place in the rocker, not saying a thing, while I carried on. Then I got going about Mama.

"That bird-legged dentist Dr. Tyler is trying a fast one, what with my daddy being missing and all. Mama's just not herself. I figure she must be sick with worrying. You've got to get that army of yours to find Daddy real fast."

Mr. Truman looked dog tired. Lately, fellows on the radio had been saying hateful things and calling him names.

"Must be real hard being president sometimes, even if you can take a train anytime or anywhere you want, or give people orders and they have to do what you say."

"You know, Annie Leigh, sometimes it's plain awful. You don't get a lot of people thanking you for being president. Our little visits are just the ticket. Walla Walla is full of nice folks. Lots of warm summer evenings, and I do like to feast my eyes on those fine Blue Mountains from time to time."

Mr. Truman's voice trailed off some. I figured he was really thinking about Missouri. He took a deck of cards out of his pocket. Seemed impolite to tell him Grandma didn't allow card-playing in her house.

I pulled a chair up next to him and watched him shuffle the cards on the cherry wood side table, his thumbs working them into a blur.

"Staying here with your Grandma isn't the worst turn of events," he continued. "Think of all that ice cream you've got left to eat." His eyes twinkled, big blue marbles behind those thick glasses of his. "Now don't you go worrying about your daddy. He'll be back. I gol' darn guarantee it." He nudged the cards my direction. "Here, cut the deck and pay attention. I'm going to teach you a card game."

The next morning Miss Gloria brought down a pan of freshly baked butterscotch rolls and found me still in my pajamas. Couldn't rustle myself out of the tangle of sheets.

She helped me put up the Murphy bed. By the time we got down to those rolls, I was itching to tell her about Daddy and Mr. Truman and a card game that was all about pairs and big houses and a bunch of flushes.

"Can you keep a secret?" I asked her.

Miss Gloria's face broke into one of her smiles. "Who would I tell?"

"Mr. Truman himself is going to find my daddy for me."

Her eyes danced, and the corners of her mouth started to twitch.

"Grandma thinks it's real silly, me talking to the president all the time." I noticed Miss Gloria couldn't seem to stop smiling.

"But as soon as Mr. Truman found out the Army lost Daddy, he promised to help."

"Uh-huh," said Miss Gloria. Her mouth was doing that twitching thing again. "I tell you what." She stopped and waited. I was sure she was about to say, "Excuse me, Annie Leigh Howard, but I seem to be having a conversation with a five-year old with an imaginary friend who is the President of the United States, no less." But when Miss Gloria opened her mouth again, she said nothing of the sort.

What she did say was, "After I finish my accounts and you have a bite of lunch, I think we should just have us a nice walk down to the picture show."

Without so much as missing a beat — in case she might change her mind — I said, "That sounds swell. Can we see *National Velvet*? It's playing at the Liberty."

We had ourselves a real nice walk. The sun was fierce, but Miss Gloria found lots of shady spots along the way. When we walked by Opal Bailey's house, she gave us a wave from her big front porch and invited us up for a cool glass of lemonade. And old Opal didn't once spit into the rose bushes while we were there. Expect she was being polite on account of Miss Gloria. Too bad, I was waiting to see if she could spit as far as the bird bath.

Grandma had made it clear we didn't have to hurry home, so on our way back from the show, Miss Gloria and I stopped at the Creamery for banana splits. I was real sorry we got there just when they were closing the counter. Miss Gloria got a funny look on her face, so I guess she was real disappointed, too. I bought us each a banana Popsicle instead.

Miss Gloria took a few tiny licks before she said anything. "You know, I used to ride horses back in Georgia. But, my land, that seems like a long time ago, and I wasn't half so grand as that little actress, Elizabeth Taylor."

"You never did tell me your story," I said, remembering our day at the creek. "Are horses part of it?" I bit off chunks of my Popsicle and sucked in my cheeks against the cold.

"I suppose they are." A big chunk of her Popsicle slid down her hand and onto the ground, and we both started to laugh.

"Eat both sides together real fast," I said. "Otherwise it just melts and gets mushy." Miss Gloria nodded and looked surprised, like I'd just said something she'd never thought of before.

"Did you have a horse in Georgia?" I asked. We were just about at the old junkyard when I heard a lot of scuffling noises and laughing, but I didn't think a thing of it. Miss Gloria was finally getting to her story.

Someone had come out from behind one of the buildings and was walking behind us. Miss Gloria linked her arm through mine to move us out of the way. Before she could answer me, Ben Jackson stood right in front of us, blocking our way. He was slapping a belt against the palm of his hand. I was mad and scared all at the same time. What did Ben Jackson think he was doing? It was broad daylight, and he was acting like a thug.

"Well, well, what have we here?" He circled us, slapping the belt the whole time. "What do you think you're doing, walking down our streets just like regular folks?"

"What are you talking about? We've been to the picture show at the Liberty." I said and backed up against Miss Gloria. "Wait 'til I tell my Grandma. She'll call the police on you."

Ben Jackson straddled the sidewalk and stared at Miss

Gloria. One of his eyes was all ringed with grease. He looked like a pirate. "You better watch that mouth, kid."

"Please move out of our way," said Miss Gloria. "I have to get Miss Annie home for her supper." She was cool as a cucumber.

Ben Jackson didn't move out of the way; he moved closer and grabbed my arm. "You run home now. This one and I have some things to talk over."

Ben Jackson was hurting my arm, and he smelled like he hadn't had a bath in a year.

"Let go of me!" I yelled. Before he knew what hit him, I punched him hard with both fists. The Popsicle stick was still in my hand, so he got a good hard poke smack in the middle of his stomach. He let out a gasp.

"You're a real polecat, aren't you, kid?" He swung the belt around and aimed for my legs. "See how you like this!"

Miss Gloria pulled me around behind her and caught the belt across her raised arm. She stumbled, and the belt caught her again, across the back.

"Hey there, what's going on?" Two men were coming across the street in our direction. It was Mr. Teeples and Reverend Wakefield, the Baptist preacher.

"Now you, young man, you stop right now, this instant!" The preacher was long on words as usual. But Ben Jackson slipped around the corner and down the alley before the end of the sentence.

Mr. Teeples put his arm around Miss Gloria's waist, kind of holding her up. "I think she's had the wind knocked out of her," he said.

"Here, sit down on the curb, Miss Washington, and catch your breath." Mr. Teeples put down a big blue farmer's hanky for Miss Gloria to sit on.

"Are you all right, Annie?" The Reverend took my hand in his.

"I'm okay, but I think Miss Gloria's hurt."

Miss Gloria struggled to her feet and wobbled a little.

"I'm just fine." She brushed off her skirt and straightened her blouse. "I think we'd better get back. Missus Howard will be worried." Her words came out in little bubbly sounds, like she was talking under water.

"Now take it careful-like," said Mr. Teeples. "We were just on our way to the ushers' meeting at the church hall, but we'll escort you two back to Miss Hattie's."

Just as we turned the corner by Grandma's store, I spotted Uncle Billy getting out of an old beat-up Ford. Since he didn't own a car, I wondered just whose car it was.

"You best come here, Annie," he said. Billy was dead set on bossing me around.

"Will not." I wanted to give him some sass, but something in his voice made the hairs on the back of my neck prickle.

"Evening, Reverend." Billy's voice was all high and snooty, like he was talking though his nose. Not polite at all, more like he was making fun of the preacher. He crossed the street and, golly, if a cigarette wasn't dangling out of the corner of his mouth. Billy stubbed it out right at the preacher's feet.

"Now, see here," said Mr. Teeples. "We need to get these two back to your Mama's."

"Look, old man. These two are my responsibility." Billy gave Mr. Teeples a little shove. "There's sure a lot of people sticking their noses into my business."

"I will not stand here and be insulted by your bad manners, Billy Howard," said the Reverend. "Now Orville and I are going to escort Miss Washington and young Annie across the street to your mother's. Please stand aside."

Uncle Billy waggled a finger at Miss Gloria. "One of

these days," he said. Then he crossed the street and got into the driver's side of the Ford and started the engine.

And didn't Ben Jackson's head pop up out of the back seat! He climbed over and into the passenger side and let his arm dangle out the window real casual-like. He gave us a pretend salute, and a big old smirk spread across his face. What a slug! Bet he'd been hiding there the whole time.

What I couldn't figure out was why Billy was hanging around with Ben Jackson at all. It hurt my heart to think Billy might have watched us being bullied without moving an inch to help. He'd always watched out for me. When everyone else used to tease me about being scared of monsters and bogeymen, it was always Billy who came and checked under the bed and looked in the closet.

Something so terrible must have happened in that war that an impostor had come back wearing Billy's skin. So I made a promise right there and then. I, Annie Leigh Howard, was going to do my most powerful best to find the real and true Billy M. Howard hiding under that tough old hide. Otherwise Daddy would come home to find a brother who was no more than a handful of red dust.

Chapter 9

The very next day Grandma moved me into Miss Gloria's apartment, and Miss Gloria moved into the apartment that had been Billy's. I was real happy to sleep in Daddy's old feather bed out on the sun porch. A locksmith came and changed all the locks and put new latches on the windows. Everyone was tiptoeing around, practically talking in whispers, but I knew a thing or two. Grandma didn't trust Ben Jackson and she most likely wasn't too sure about Billy, either.

Reverend Wakefield and a stranger in a dark suit with a face like Opal Bailey's hound arrived after lunch. Grandma showed them into the dining room, so I knew it was serious business. No one was allowed in the dining room except at Christmas. Once I looked in and saw the

Reverend pacing up and down, shaking his head like a squirrel had a hold of his ear and wouldn't let go. The stranger was listening real hard and writing in a little black notebook.

When an hour had gone by and the doors were still closed, I cracked open the door to see what was going on. The Reverend was still pacing. Grandma got a glimpse of me and fanned her hand at me to move, but I stayed where I was and gave her my fiercest stare. She finally came to the door.

"What is it, Annie Leigh?"

"How come the Reverend is here in the middle of the day? And who is that man with all the chins?"

"Don't be rude, Annie." Grandma let out one of her big sighs. "If you must know, Miss Nosy, Reverend Wakefield was concerned about us, so he brought that nice officer over to talk about what happened yesterday. Now scoot."

She fanned her hand at me again. This time I went.

I found Miss Gloria back in the little office off the kitchen. I pulled up a footstool and sat down to talk.

"There's a man in the dining room with Grandma and the Reverend," I said. "He's a policeman."

Miss Gloria didn't respond. She kept her head bent over the accounts.

"I hope he puts ol' Ben Jackson in jail and scares the poop out of Uncle Billy."

Then Miss Gloria turned to look at me with that funny cockeyed smile she got sometimes. "I wouldn't say that in front of your Grandma, Annie."

Her mouth started to do that twitching thing it always did when she was trying hard not to laugh. I pulled my footstool over closer to the desk.

"I sure wish my Daddy would come home." I decided I'd finally have me a heart-to-heart with Miss Gloria. "No one around here ever talks about Daddy 'cause they think he isn't coming back, but I know he will. Mr. Truman says so, too."

Miss Gloria reached for my hand and gave it a pat. "No harm in having faith that he's alive," she said.

"Whenever I try to talk to Grandma about Daddy, she talks around in a big circle like I'm too little to understand."

"Grownups don't like to talk about the sad things." Miss Gloria stopped to pull her sleeve down over her wrist, but I'd already seen the nasty welt that ran like a stripe

68

clear up to her elbow. "Sometimes you need to put things you don't want to think about in a secret place for a while, where no one can touch them, not even you."

I was pretty sure Miss Gloria wasn't just talking about Grandma.

"Staying here with Grandma's not so bad, but I don't want to start a new school year and have to meet a whole lot of new kids. I already missed a bunch of school because of my appendix. What if I can't keep up?"

I didn't give Miss Gloria a chance to answer. There was so much on my mind.

"I should be home with Mama," I went on. "I can't figure out why she wants me to stay in Walla Walla for the whole school year. Do you suppose her heart is so heavy missing Daddy she can't think straight?"

"Now, now, Annie. Don't fret so," said Miss Gloria. "Everything will turn out just fine. Making friends is the easiest thing in the world. You'll see. And as for your mama, I hear she's got herself a new job. She's going to be settling you all in a spanking new place, too. She probably needs some time to work all that out."

"Miss Gloria, can your heart really and truly break?"

"Oh, child," she said.

And then she did something that truly surprised me. She grabbed my arms and pulled me up into a big violet smelling hug. I hugged her right back, and before I could stop them, a whole bunch of tears were rolling down my face.

"Hush, child, hush." Miss Gloria began to hum ever so softly. We just stood there for the longest time and she held onto me real tight while I cried big wet blotches all over her blouse.

Crying was something I didn't do much. But somehow crying in front of Miss Gloria let me get out a big bunch of sorrow I didn't know I had. After a while, she took her hanky and rinsed it out in cold water and had me hold it over my eyes. She stroked my head and rubbed my neck until I got to the stage where I was just gulping air.

"You wait here a minute." And in two shakes Miss Gloria was back with some of her violet perfume. She put two tiny dabs behind each of my ears.

"Now then," she said. "We'll just give your hair a brush, and the world won't even know about all those tears."

After that day, even though I had slobbered all over her, Miss Gloria let me sit in the little office as much as I liked, as long as I didn't bother her when she was doing her numbers.

One Monday morning, about a week before school started, I was reading a Nancy Drew and Miss Gloria was concentrating on the accounts real hard like always. I started thinking about Daddy, and a nasty lump started to wiggle its way into my throat.

The night before, I'd cuddled next to Daddy's old quilt and tried to find his smell among the blankets. I got up and looked in the closet, hoping to find just a sniff of soap or peppermint — something to help me remember his smiling face. Nothing of his was there, so I had to settle for stroking the silky smooth wood of the chest of drawers he'd made with his own two hands. He was the best carpenter in Seattle. Everybody said so. Daddy had to come back soon, or before long his face might get all blurry in my head, and his voice barely a whisper.

"A penny for your thoughts." Miss Gloria took off her glasses and folded them into a silver case. "Your pretty face is all clouded over with a frown."

"When I try to picture Daddy's face, I have a hard time seeing him," I said. "His smile is still there, but sometimes the edges are all funny, like when the picture shows are out of focus."

"Time has a way of doing that," said Miss Gloria, "but you can look at snapshots and think about the good times."

"I have a picture of Daddy right by my bed. He's holding me up by my heels and his face is all smiles."

So that's how Miss Gloria and I ended up in the kitchen with our family photos all over the kitchen table. Mine were in an old cigar box and Miss Gloria kept hers in a cracker tin. We got to giggling about the silly ones, and she admired the one of Daddy in his uniform. She was tickled that we both had pictures taken of us sitting on shaggy old ponies.

"Those sad critters," she said. "If I didn't know better, I'd say you and I were photographed on the same poor old pony!" Miss Gloria shuffled through the tin and handed me a photo of a handsome young man with smiling eyes. He was in uniform, too.

"Who is this?" I asked. "He has a kind face."

"Oh, indeed," said Miss Gloria. "He was the kindest soul I ever did know."

"Is he back home in Georgia?"

"Well, yes, he is. He's in his final resting place, and I believe he's at peace now." Miss Gloria had those sad eyes again. There was nothing I could do but give her hand a real soft squeeze.

While we were looking at pictures, the sun had dropped and the room was full of shadows and long strips of light. Fall was on its way for sure. The room was so quiet that a pin dropping would have made me cover my ears. Miss Gloria stood up and went to look out the back door. I figured she was trying to see all the way to Georgia. I stayed until she felt like talking again. Finally she was getting to her story.

"Robert James Brooks," said Miss Gloria, finally. "That was his name, but everyone called him R.J. We were planning to be married."

"What happened?" I asked her in the softest voice possible. "How did you get all the way to Walla Walla?"

"His company was assigned to a base here at the end of the war, but he never even made it to his troop ship alive." Gloria let out a big sigh. "I just decided to come out West anyway and try to live the life we planned. I never intended to stay in Walla Walla necessarily. But the train had a long stop here, so I took me a stroll around and liked what I saw."

"And then you met Grandma and me," I said.

"That I did," said Miss Gloria. "That I did."

I knew better than to say much more, so I just sat there with Miss Gloria and watched the rest of the day fade away.

I took the stairs up to Daddy's room real slow. My feet were full of lead. It seemed to me too many folks were awful sad and lonely or else angry about something, like the war hadn't truly ended. Little bits and pieces of it were still stuck in everybody's craw like a tiny bit of fish bone. Not nearly enough to choke you to death but enough to make your throat raw.

Chapter 10

One thing I knew for sure: I wasn't in a big hurry to grow up. Adults never seemed to have much fun. When they could be doing neat things like riding Ferris wheels and eating cotton candy or roller skating, they used up their energy finding fault with folks and starting wars. Or else they sat around and talked and talked and nothing much ever got settled. Didn't make a whole lot of sense to me.

"To me either, Annie Leigh," said a familiar voice.

"You liked to scared me to death, sir."

"Sorry if I startled you. I couldn't help but overhear that last remark." Mr. Truman was sitting at his piano looking out across the back yard. "Must be nice going to sleep in your daddy's room with the sound of that creek water in your ear."

It occurred to me I hadn't been talking to myself out loud.

"How'd you know what I was thinking?"

"Now, Annie Leigh, you know I've got my very own pass key into that head of yours."

That didn't quite make sense to me, but I was ready to burst with all the things I had to tell him.

"Seems to me there's too many bullies around, mean folks who go around making trouble for good people. Look at what's happened to Billy. Goodness knows what ugliness he's up to. Here it is almost the end of August, and we haven't seen him in ages. Please don't think he's always been up to no good. Sure, he used to drive Grandma to distraction bringing home all those stray dogs, but he never brought around sorry folks like Ben Jackson."

I knew I was rambling on, but Mr. Truman seemed to hang on every word, so I kept on talking.

"Maybe he and that ornery ol' Ben Jackson have walked to the ends of the earth and just fallen right off the edge. And have you noticed? Miss Gloria's got the saddest eyes you ever did see, and the worry lines in Grandma's face just keep getting deeper and deeper. Mama's probably forgotten about me, and still no word from Daddy. So it's up to me to make things peaceful, and that sure is hard work."

"That's a lot to carry around, Annie Leigh. You might try letting other folks help you with the weight of it." Mr. Truman had been playing with the keys of his big white piano all this time. I was real happy he'd brought it along with him. He shook his head and played a few chords.

"Guess toting this thing around is hard on it," he said. "Darn piano needs tuning again." He ran his fingers down the length of the keys, played a few notes, and then stopped.

"Here's the thing, Annie Leigh. You're right. Fighting people doesn't make a whole lot of sense, and I can't say to you we'll never be at war again. I mean, look here, you got people around who didn't give it a second thought before striking your Miss Gloria. But you got to believe that most folks are basically good people. You stop believing that, and you might as well give up on the whole lot of us. Sometimes it takes seeing things from the other fellow's point of view. See if you can figure out what makes Billy tick. Most likely, you'll find some answers there."

Mr. Truman fiddled with the piano keys some more and then played a piece that had all kinds of chords. His hands flew up and down that piano so fast, I got dizzy watching him.

"Not bad, not bad, if I do say so myself," he said and closed the piano with a thud. Then he tipped his hat at me and was gone. He sailed right through the window screen and off across the creek, pulling the piano behind him.

Someone began to whistle. Couldn't remember ever hearing the president whistle before.

"Get up, sleepyhead." It was Grandma standing in the doorway. "My land, you were dead to the world! But you've got a big day ahead of you. We're going shopping. Thought we'd go downtown and buy you some school clothes, act like fine ladies, and treat ourselves to lunch at the Marcus Whitman Hotel. Goodness knows, we deserve it."

Shopping wasn't my favorite thing to do, but the whole idea seemed to lift Grandma's spirits. Besides, it had been a long time since I'd had Grandma to myself for a whole day. She was also probably thinking that my birthday was just days away.

"I'll go tell Scooter he's in charge today and then change my dress," said Grandma. "It's too hot to walk, so we'll take the bus. And wear that lovely dress of yours with the apple blossoms on it."

Miss Gloria was in the kitchen mixing pancakes when I came down. I was fussing with the sash on my dress and she came over to tie it before I made a mess of things.

"Starting a new school is the worst! I'll be the new kid. I hate that! Just wait, the teacher will make me sit by the biggest pest in class. I hadn't figured on staying at Grandma's, so all my school clothes are still at home. Mama always makes a big thing out of shopping for school clothes, too. Why the fuss over a bunch of scratchy old sweaters and stiff old oxfords? Why can't I wear jeans or overalls to school?"

Miss Gloria didn't say a thing. She was busy pouring batter over the griddle, so I kept rattling on. I was really getting worked up.

"I need to be figuring out how to get my daddy home, and here I am fussing over a new school and new clothes instead."

Miss Gloria put a plate of pancakes in front of me with a thunk, all the while making tsk-tsk noises. I figured she'd heard enough when her hands went to her hips and she gave her head a little shake.

"Why, I swear, Miss Annie Leigh, I never heard you whine like that. Go on, now, eat your breakfast. You'll have yourself a fine day."

Grandma decided since we were in our Sunday best, taking the bus just wouldn't do, and she called us a cab. We started off by stepping out in front of Mason's Mercantile like we were the Rockefellers. From then on Grandma set a fast pace, and I figured we must have bought out the town. The best part was when the waiter at the hotel called me "Miss" and brought me a finger bowl. Grandma and I talked and laughed and even had chocolate parfaits for dessert. Miss Gloria was right, we did have us a fine day.

By the time we got back home, I was dead tired and ready for an ice-cold soda pop. We had boxes of stuff. New blouses and pleated skirts and a new red coat, and even patent leather shoes.

"Those are to be saved for church," Grandma said. I was thankful she never mentioned the oxfords. But I had been forced to get a fuzzy pink sweater Grandma had her heart set on. I wasn't about to tell her I'd wear a burlap vegetable bag before I'd put on a prissy thing like that.

Miss Gloria met us at the door. "My, you two must

have had yourselves a grand time." She took my armload of boxes and followed me into the living room. After Grandma left to change her shoes, Gloria handed me an envelope.

"This came for your grandma today." She looked about to burst. "I think it's something important."

The envelope was big and looked real important. I read the name on the return address. Major Jack Wilson.

"My land, child, I wish your grandma would hurry up!" Miss Gloria twisted her hanky into a big knot.

My knees suddenly got all wobbly, and I had to sit down.

"What are you two going on about?" Grandma said, walking into the living room.

"I think you need to open this, Missus Howard." Gloria handed her the letter.

Grandma picked at the seal so slowly, I was about to jump up and yank it out of her hand. I watched her eyes skim over the words real fast. When she finished, her hand flew up to her throat.

"Oh, my!" she exclaimed. "Oh, my!"

The next few minutes were a jumble of words. Miss Gloria and I both started with all kinds of questions, not bothering to wait for the other to finish. Finally, Grandma put her hand up.

"Wait, you two," she said. "I can scarcely get my breath." She dabbed at her eyes with the end of her apron.

"Now, this is from a pilot who served with your daddy. He begins by telling me he's been in the hospital for the better part of a year, and has only recently been well enough to write." Grandma cleared her throat. "Seems he had my address because he and your daddy had made a promise to each other, that if . . ."

At this point Grandma was swallowing hard and had to stop for a minute. "Major Wilson and your daddy had promised each other that if anything happened to the other, the one left would personally get in touch with his family. He tried to send word to your mama, but that letter was returned. He apologizes that it's taken so long, but his injuries were such that he was unable to fulfill that promise until now."

"Does he know what happened to Daddy?" I was all pins and needles.

Grandma stayed quiet for a moment. Then she began to read: "Mrs. Howard, I want you to know that Eddie is the bravest man I know, and the kind of guy who could get himself out of any fix he found himself in. I can tell you that my plane was in the air when his got hit and he got out of there before it went down. I saw his chute open. Don't give up hope. I haven't. It's a promise. I will make every effort to find out what happened."

The three of us sat staring at the letter, unable to speak. It was certainly time for the Orange Crush. Before Grandma could say a word, I ran into the store and grabbed three ice-cold bottles.

The room was quiet as a church when I came back. The smile on Gloria's face had faded, and Grandma waved off the Orange Crush I held out.

"I'll have mine later," she said. "I've got to ring your mama."

"I want to talk to her, too."

Grandma just shook her head. "We'll see. Maybe later." She handed me the letter and then turned away and hurried into the back hall. The letter felt hot in my hand. I wasn't sure I really and truly wanted to read it myself.

I took a big swallow of Orange Crush that went down the wrong way, and Miss Gloria had to thump me on the back until I stopped coughing.

"Is Grandma awful upset?"

Miss Gloria motioned for me to follow her over to the couch and patted the spot next to her. "She's got some thinking to do. Your grandma had made her peace with your daddy being missing and all. It's real hard for a person to bring up those feelings all over again. Now, read me that letter out loud. Everything that major wrote."

She nodded and made humming sounds the whole time. "Now isn't that something. You'll have to write that Major Wilson a letter. That was real kind of him to write to you all." Gloria leaned closer and looked straight into my face like she thought she might find something there.

"Ever have your eyes tested at school?" she asked. "You were holding that letter awful close to your face, child."

I looked down at the letter. The words all kind of blurred together. They wouldn't stay still. "The letters got all fuzzy 'cause my eyes got wet."

"I think you might need glasses, sweet thing." Gloria gave my shoulder a little pat. "I'll have a little talk with your grandma tonight."

"Don't need glasses," I said and stomped off to see if I could talk to Mama. I could hear Miss Gloria let out a big sigh.

I could just see myself, the new ugly city kid at school.

Big pink puffy sweater, wretched old glasses, and oxfords. I wouldn't have a friend in the world! I decided I'd have to practice so I could read that letter without tucking it practically under my nose. Then everyone could forget about eyeglasses. Bet Mama wouldn't make me get glasses or wear puffy sweaters.

I took the letter to bed with me and put it under my pillow. I was jealous of Major Wilson's kids. They knew where their daddy was. I lay there for the longest time and thought about all the things we'd do when Daddy got back. First thing, we'd get Grandpa's old pickup running and race it in and out of the abandoned plum orchards.

My thoughts were interrupted by loud shuffling sounds outside. I lay real still and listened. Somebody was hammering something, but I couldn't quite make out what. There was something peculiar about it. A little shiver ran up and down my spine, and my arm broke out all over in goose bumps. For just a brief second I could smell something strong — kerosene or maybe gasoline.

Then all of a sudden there was a big whoosh. Bright red and yellow flames began to dance outside my window. I froze for a minute. Then Miss Gloria burst into my room.

She grabbed me out of bed in one fell swoop and threw a blanket around my shoulders.

"Grandma," I yelled, "the house is on fire! We got to get out!"

We hurried downstairs to get Grandma, but she was already on the phone to the fire department.

Gloria had let go of my hand and was staring out the front window.

"The one thing we don't want to do is go outside," Miss Gloria said. "Look!"

Grandma put the phone down and followed her to the window. There in the front yard, right in the middle of Grandma's rose garden, was a giant cross, all ablaze. The flames climbed higher and higher upwards until they lit up the night sky like some kind of evil Fourth of July prank.

"Good Lord!" gasped Miss Gloria. Her voice was low and shaky. "This is only the second time I've seen one of those, and I never thought to see one out West."

Grandma put her arm around Miss Gloria and stood silently, shaking her head. Sirens wailed in the distance.

"Is it the end of the world, Grandma? Is the devil out there?"

"It's not the end of the world, child," said Grandma, "but you can be sure this is the work of the worst kind of devil. A cowardly one."

Then she re-pinned her hair, pulled her bathrobe around her tightly, and went out on the front porch to meet the fireman coming up the walk.

Chapter 11

No one slept a wink the rest of the night. If I tried to close my eyes, they just popped right back open like a baby doll's. How could a person sleep? The house smelled of wet ashes and garbage dumps. The stink made my eyes water and my chest hurt. There were policemen everywhere, asking questions and telling people not to walk on Grandma's lawn.

One policeman came right into the house and started asking me questions. He asked me the same question three times, three different ways. Did I hear anything? What kind of noise was it? Was it a loud sound or a soft one? When I told him about the hammering noise, he asked me to tell him what it sounded like.

"Like someone using a hammer," I told him. Pretty

dumb, someone not knowing what kind of noise a hammer makes. He didn't seem to have good sense. Gloria was standing right there, too, but he kept asking me to ask her the same questions.

"She talks, you know," I said.

The policeman tugged at his tie and pulled at his collar like he had an itch.

"I'm Missus Howard's bookkeeper," said Miss Gloria, and she gave my arm a squeeze. "What would you like to know?"

I left Miss Gloria to talk to the policeman and went over to the front window. Mrs. Hawkins and a handful of neighbors were still out in the street in their nightclothes. Everyone was talking at once and waving their arms around and pointing fingers.

Grandma was sitting in one of the porch chairs having a real serious conversation with the Reverend. I didn't want to look at what was left of the cross. Instead, I studied the sky. Little slivers of light showed through the trees. It would soon be daylight. In all my life I had never stayed up for almost a whole night.

Just as the sun burst through the trees, I fell asleep scrunched into the corner of the sofa. I thought I could have stayed there for a year, but the phone started ringing and woke me up. If my leg hadn't fallen completely asleep, I would have run into the hall to answer it. Gloria had been dozing in Grandma's favorite chair. She sat up with a start and began rubbing her neck to get the kinks out. Out in the hall Grandma's voice rose and fell in little waves of excitement. I couldn't make out a word.

Most times when the phone rang, I wished real hard it would be Mama calling. Today was different. Last thing in the world I wanted was to give her one more thing to worry about.

Miss Gloria looked at her watch. "For pity sakes, it's almost noon. We've gone and slept right through church!"

Someone began to pound on the back door. I got up to answer it, but Miss Gloria said she'd go. For a minute my heart did a little flippity-flop. I followed Gloria into the kitchen. No old devil boys were going to scare me.

"Look what Miss Bailey's brought us." Miss Gloria was holding a basket the size of a dishpan full of cinnamon rolls. At least I sure hoped that was cinnamon on the top of the rolls and not specks of Opal Bailey's tobacco juice.

"Homemade cinnamon buns," Miss Bailey said. "Baked them myself this mornin'."

I scrunched up my nose, and Miss Gloria gave me a look.

"Thank you kindly, Ma'am," said Miss Gloria. "That's real sweet."

Opal Bailey had scarcely left when Mr. Teeples came by, a bunch of the church ushers right behind him. Every last one of them was carrying a dish of something.

"Mornin', Annie." Mr. Teeples put a boiled ham down on the kitchen table. "Mornin', Miss Washington." He took off his hat and worried the brim some before he figured out just what he wanted to say.

"I think some of the good people of Walla Walla are feeling rather shamefaced about what happened in our little town last night." He stopped to clear a big frog out of his throat. "We figured when you didn't make it to church this morning, we'd just dang well bring the congregation to you."

"I'm much obliged." Miss Gloria offered her hand, and Mr. Teeples gave it a quick shake and shuffled out into the living room.

"I'd best put on a pot of coffee," said Miss Gloria. "Annie, you'd better get out all the cups and saucers you can find."

91

Pretty soon most of the choir arrived, and the living room was brimming over with all kinds of folks.

"For land sakes!" said Grandma when she saw all the people. "Where did you all come from?" She had a funny look on her face and stood there fussing with a hanky. Her eyes were real droopy. I figured she just as soon everyone left us in peace.

"Open the doors into the dining room, Annie," she said. "We can't have people sitting in each other's laps."

Then Gloria waved me into the kitchen, and I helped her take the salads and cakes and sandwiches into the dining room. I took another look at Miss Bailey's cinnamon rolls — I still wasn't convinced I was looking at cinnamon. I put my nose real close to those buns and took a big sniff.

"Annie Leigh Howard, what in the world are you doing?" Grandma had a stack of her best Sunday dishes in her hands. "Get your nose out of those rolls!"

"Just checking, Grandma."

I was saved from more eye rolling from Grandma by a stream of hungry people. Once those plates were down, folks couldn't get to the table fast enough. I fixed a plate for myself and had just started chewing a mouthful of potato salad when Reverend Wakefield called for silence so we could say grace.

"Miss Annie, you have a lot to thank the Lord for today," he said. "Why don't you say the blessing?"

Darn if I didn't almost choke on a piece of potato! I'd been hoping no one saw me over in the corner. I chewed real fast and swallowed, but the potato got stuck halfway down. Everyone was looking at me, so I had to say something.

"Dear Lord," I began. The words barely squeaked out. That piece of potato wouldn't budge. I swallowed hard and began again. "Dear Lord, thank you for all this good food." Grandma was standing in the doorway with a platter of sandwiches in her hand. She nodded for me to go on.

"And another thing, Lord, you find those devil boys and make them clean up the mess, and tell Grandma they're sorry." I said the last part so fast I was out of breath. I took a big gulp of air. "And another thing, please. If you could make this stink go away, I'd appreciate it. Amen."

A big chorus of "Amens" went around the room.

I went back to my plate, and people kept coming by and patting my head and pinching my cheeks and calling me "Sweetie." It was time to go into the kitchen where I could have some peace and quiet. I hadn't been there five minutes when Uncle Billy came from behind the garden shed and then stopped at the end of the walk to light a cigarette. What did he want?

I unlatched the screen, on my way out the back door to give him what-for, when I saw Grandma coming in for the lemonade.

"Look, Grandma, there's Billy." I hoped she'd go out there and give him a piece of her mind.

"My stars," said Grandma. "Of all days."

She called out to Billy from the back steps. He slunk across the backyard like a sorry ol' tom cat. His clothes were all dirty and rumpled, and he had a face full of whiskers. He looked like a tramp.

"Good heavens, son!" Grandma's face got all bunched up. She most likely was thinking hard about what to say next.

"Where you been?" I asked. "Someone tried to burn the house down."

"You all right, Ma?" Uncle Billy studied his shoes for a while, then looked at me. "Don't believe the house was in any serious danger."

"Well, it was very frightening nonetheless," said Grandma.

"You got to get rid of that girl," said Billy. "She's going to bring you nothing but grief."

I walked down the steps and marched right over to him.

"If you mean Miss Gloria, she's my very best friend. Why, she's acting more like family than you are. You're just about the meanest person in the world! I think Grandma ought to take you out to the shed and give you a good whippin' and then wash your mouth out with soap."

"That's a good one," said Billy. "You're the one needs a good whippin'. That mouth of yours is going to get you into a whole lot of trouble one of these days."

All this time Grandma looked like she wanted to cry.

"You know something about who did this, don't you, son?" Grandma folded her arms and waited for an answer.

"Can't say that I do, Ma, but a whole lot of people are unhappy about you allowing colored to live in our house."

"There's a whole room full of fine people in my house right now," said Grandma. "And not a one of them has voiced an objection to Gloria living here." She couldn't keep the shakes out of her voice, but she held her ground.

"You mean those church folks?" said Billy. "What do they know about anything?"

"I think they know a strong Christian woman when they have the good fortune to meet one. If you care about me, and Annie, your own brother's child, you'll go to the police with whatever you know."

Grandma came down the steps and took my hand and walked me back up to the kitchen door. Before she went on in, she turned back to face Billy.

"Meanwhile, William, unless you can act like a civil human being, you can just make yourself scarce around here."

Billy was quiet for a full minute. Then he looked up at Grandma and gave her one of his nasty smirks. "I don't particularly care to be here anyway, Ma. I just stopped by to see if I could talk some sense into you."

I started to say something, but Grandma tugged on my arm. We stood there watching him lope across the lawn and finally disappear behind the garage.

Back in the kitchen, the flies were making a feast out of my lunch. I wasn't hungry anymore, anyhow. Grandma went into the pantry and closed the door. Pretty soon I could hear her crying her eyes out. Most times I would've gone in and given her a hug or maybe rubbed her back. This time I just sat at the table and listened. Her heart must have nearly cracked in two when Daddy went missing. And now Uncle Billy had turned out to be more than mean. Grandma's heart was in a million pieces, and I didn't know how to begin to put it back together.

Chapter 12

Come Monday morning, it felt like the whole town was still wandering through Grandma's living room. When all those voices began to buzz in my head like a bunch of bees, I sneaked back up to my room. It still smelled like a garbage dump. Out by the creek was the only place where person could find a little peace and quiet, without the stink. And that's where Mr. Truman found me.

"Annie Leigh, I dropped everything when I got your message. Got here as soon as I could. Terrible business. Terrible."

I had never seen the president in his shirtsleeves before, or with suspenders flapping at his sides, for that matter. He sure must have left the White House in one big hurry. Guess he caught me staring 'cause he snapped those suspenders up on his shoulders and started apologizing all over the place. Before I could say a word, he started to roll down his sleeves and apologize some more.

"I was right in the middle of my morning shave when I learned of your distress," he said. "Well, it seemed to me there was nothing to be done but come right out and see how you were doing."

And then if he didn't sit right down next to me on the grass. I bet Bess didn't yell at him about grass stains the way Mama did with me.

"I don't think I've ever been so scared," I said, lowering my voice a little. Wouldn't do to add to Grandma's worries. And it wasn't like me to tell folks when something frightened me, but I knew Harry S. Truman would keep personal things to himself.

"I was awful scared the house was going to burn right down, with us in it. Someone must hate Grandma real bad. How could anyone be so wicked? Some people are just real stinkers."

"It's a hard truth to discover that there are truly hateful folks out in the world, but I figure you knew that already." Mr. Truman let out a funny kind of laugh. "Let me tell you, some of them have their sights set on me." Then he jumped up and slapped at his trouser legs.

"Annie Leigh, this whole business stinks like a huge pile of horse manure, but I do believe you are one of the toughest little ladies I know. You're doing right well for someone who's had such a scare. Just remember, let me know, and I'll be back at the first sign of trouble."

And then he did that trick where he floated off across the creek. One of these days I was going to get him to show me how he did that.

"What are you doing, child?" It was Miss Gloria, come to look for me. "Why are you out here talking to yourself? Everyone's been asking for you." She sat down beside me and smoothed out her skirt.

"Like who?"

"Well, Scooter, for one. He said you didn't take the bags off the vegetables this morning."

"Forgot."

"I think you can be excused this morning," said Miss Gloria. "You can't help but be forgetful after such an awful fright, especially one that that raises a person right out of a sound sleep."

"Who'd want to harm Grandma? Uncle Billy's been an

awful pill, but do you think he would really and truly hurt his own mama?"

"Oh, sweet thing." Miss Gloria let out one of her long sighs. I thought she was going to say something else, but she changed the subject. "You better eat some breakfast and get ready for school. You don't want to miss the whole first day."

"I wish I didn't have to go at all."

"C'mon Miss Sourpuss, go change and I'll walk you," said Miss Gloria. "Your grandma's got enough on her mind. If you like, I'll come meet you after school."

Ordinarily, I would have made a big fuss about being walked to the first day of sixth grade, but I was real happy to have someone go with me.

Over breakfast Grandma was quiet as could be. I guessed she'd forgotten all about me starting school. She probably also forgot it was also my eleventh birthday, but I didn't remind her.

Just like she promised, Miss Gloria was waiting for me at the edge of the playground when school ended.

"How did things go?" she asked. She had on one of her lavender dresses.

"Sixth grade isn't so bad. My teacher's name is Miss Dibble." I couldn't say the name without giggling. "Can you imagine that?"

Gloria put two fingers up to my lips and gave me one of her looks.

"You know what else?" I said. "She wears her glasses around her neck like a string of pearls, and she rings this little bell when she wants our attention. And oh boy! Those kids sit up straight as yardsticks when that little bell rings."

"I bet you met lots of new friends," said Miss Gloria.

Before I could answer, the curly top who sat in front of me and chewed her hair came running up behind us.

"Hey, new girl, wait up!" Curly huffed and puffed behind me. "Slow down, would ya?"

Miss Gloria walked ahead a ways. I stopped and put on the best mean sneer I could manage. "I have a name. It's Annie. Annie Leigh Howard to be exact."

"Well, Annie Leigh Howard, what are you doing hanging around with that colored lady?" The girl bent over and put her hands on her knees trying to catch her breath.

"She's my friend. And you must be real dumb not to see that." I turned my back on her real fast and ran to catch up with Miss Gloria.

"Why didn't you ask your friend back to the house?" said Miss Gloria. "I think your Grandma has a surprise for you."

"She's not my friend." I hoped Miss Gloria hadn't heard the girl's stupid question. "You're my friend. You're my very best friend in the whole world."

"That's a very nice thing to say, Annie," said Miss Gloria. "But you'll make new friends, lots and lots of them. You'll see."

If the kids were all like curly top, I didn't think so, but I didn't tell Miss Gloria that. Besides, I had enough on my mind without having to meet a bunch of new kids.

As soon as we turned the corner by the store, I could see paper streamers hanging from the branches of the dogwood tree. A sign directed us to go down the back walk. Good thing, too. I wasn't about to walk past the scorched rosebushes in the front yard. Folks were filing into the yard from all directions, but Grandma was nowhere in sight.

I finally found her bent over a table, putting the last of the candles on a big birthday cake.

"There's the birthday girl," she said. "Look at that face. You didn't think I'd forgotten did you?"

"Oh, Grandma, it's so beautiful!" The trees were full of bright colored streamers and paper lanterns in a rainbow of colors.

"How'd you get all those up there?"

"You have Scooter to thank for that."

I gave Scooter a wave and tried to take it all in. The side yard was full of tables covered in bright material to match the lanterns. In the center of each table, from one end to the other, were garlands of late summer flowers. Grandma picked a crown of fern and roses out of the bunch nearest her and placed it on my head.

"These are not just table decorations," she said. "You can wear them."

"You put one on, too, Gloria." I handed her a crown with lavender ribbons.

There was enough ice cream and cake to feed a kingdom. I felt like a fairy princess. Miss Gloria struck a match and lit the candles on the cake.

"Make a wish," someone yelled.

Even with all the commotion of the past few days, I hadn't forgotten about Major Wilson's letter. My biggest wish was for Daddy. In one big breath, I took care of every last candle. Everyone clapped. I cut the first piece of cake and then Gloria took over. Grandma went into the house for more forks.

"Those presents over yonder are all for you," said Miss Gloria.

"I don't even know that many people in town," I said. "Where did all those packages come from?"

"I expect these nice folks figured you deserved something real special." Miss Gloria pulled me into a hug that was all sticky with birthday frosting.

So I didn't blubber right there in front of everybody, I ran up the steps and into the kitchen before anyone saw that I was bawling like a baby. Grandma was on her way back out to the yard. I rushed right past her.

"Wait up, Sweetpea." Grandma turned right around and followed me back into the kitchen. She had her hands full of silverware, but she just dropped all the forks and spoons right in a heap on the table and opened up her arms.

"You just go ahead. Have yourself a good cry." Grandma

made a sniffling noise. "A body just has to let it all out some-times."

We stood there for the longest time holding onto each other. We didn't move an inch until Mr. Teeples came in looking for spoons.

"Sorry, Hattie. Didn't mean to interrupt." He grabbed a big bunch of silverware off the table and scurried out the back door.

"Let's go sit in the living room for a spell," said Grandma. "There's a letter for you."

My heart skipped a beat. It wasn't bad news about Daddy. Oh, please, not about Daddy!

Grandma settled herself in her chair and motioned for me to sit on the footstool in front of her. She reached into her apron pocket and brought out an envelope.

"This came today," Grandma said. "It's from your mama."

The envelope was lumpy, and it felt hot and sticky in my hand. I was almost afraid to open it.

"Why didn't she call? Seems to me a phone call from someone's mama ought to be a regular part of celebrating your birthday." I slipped the envelope into my pocket, but not before I got the tiniest whiff of her perfume, "Evening in Paris." I had to swallow hard to keep a lump from moving up my throat.

"I think I'll read it later."

"Your mama's had a lot to do lately. Most likely she doesn't have a phone in her new place yet." Grandma blew her nose and cleared her throat. "I expect it's all explained in there."

I hoped whatever was keeping Mama so busy she couldn't even call had nothing to do with that dentist on stork legs.

Grandma reached for my hands and folded them into hers. "Let's go back out to your party. There's a lot of people out there raring to show you a real fine time."

"I'll be out in a minute, Grandma."

After a while, I heard Grandma tell Scooter to get more soda pop out of the store. I knew I should go out to the party, but my body felt heavy, like to move would be the hardest thing in the world. So I opened Mama's card. A silver dollar fell out. She'd wrapped it up tight in a piece of tissue paper and tucked it inside.

"You shine just as bright as this dollar. Don't spend it all in one place," she'd written in those big round letters of hers. "Happy Birthday. Love, Mama."

Everything seemed off-kilter. Families were supposed to stick together. To look out for each other. But Daddy was still missing, Mama was too busy to write a real letter or even to call, Grandma almost had her house burned down, and near as I could tell, Billy didn't want us in his life at all.

Chapter 13

"I don't know why Billy and those terrible ol' boys are so mean to Miss Gloria. Why, she's nice as pie."

It was a Thursday night. We'd just finished going over my weekly spelling words, and I was sitting on Grandma's bed watching her carefully unwind her long silvery braid.

"At first I thought it was because she wasn't from around here, and a few sorry folks wouldn't give her a chance. But now, all I can figure is that it's 'cause she's colored . . . but that doesn't make any sense."

Thinking about all this was giving me a headache. I had about one hundred questions lining up in my brain. If I didn't get them out, I was going to burst.

"Is that why someone tried to burn the house down? Because of Miss Gloria? And how come they made a torch out of a cross?" I was really getting my dander up. "I never had any Sunday school lessons about lighting fires with a cross. Who would do such a thing?"

Grandma just kept working at the braid and gingerly loosening strands of hair. I could see her face reflected in the mirror above her dressing table. She was concentrating real hard, like getting that braid undone was the most important thing on earth.

"Now slow down, Annie Leigh. I know it's upsetting. Discovering that there are people who would actually do such terrible things is real hard. But there are folks in this world who get strange ideas in their heads about right and wrong. They twist things to fit their intentions. Like that cross. Whoever set it on fire meant to scare us. Using something we cherish, they figured they could frighten us into sending Gloria away. It breaks my heart to think we could witness such disgraceful behavior in our little town."

Grandma stayed extra quiet for a long time. I could see that talking about hateful folks made her real sad. She turned away from the mirror to face me.

"I'd like to think that our family has always accepted folks, and we don't hold any fool notions about what color they are or where they come from. But some folks get stuck in their ways. Can't abide outsiders," she said. "It's not like Billy never met a Negro before. Reverend Hubbs, that nice army chaplain who moved here during the war, he used to drop by with his two little girls for lime soda pop. Of course, can't say as the army has helped bring white and colored together. Those Negro soldiers out at the air base still have to stick pretty close to quarters and keep to themselves."

Grandma let out one of her heavy sighs. It seemed to take all her strength to go on. "I didn't bring up your uncle to hold bad feelings about people because of their color. It's got to be the war and those good-for-nothings he's be-friended. He could only survive by turning off any kind of goodness, and now he can't turn those feelings back on."

"Uncle Billy's been so mean to Gloria, but other people have been stupid too. A girl at my school was just plain rude to us other day. And come to think of it, that day at the Creamery was strange. Why, I bet that sassy girl be-hind the counter decided to close 'cause Miss Gloria was with me."

"What day was that?" Grandma was talking into the mirror, but her gaze was on me. Her hands stopped working on her hair and went to her hips. I had her full attention now. "Did they refuse to serve her?"

"It was that day Ben Jackson bullied us in the street. The girl in the Creamery said it was too late to make banana splits. How could I have been so dumb? It was too early for them to be closing. And now that I think on it, that girl only talked to me, not to Miss Gloria."

"That so! The next time I'm at a Chamber of Commerce meeting, I just might have something to say about that." Grandma finished finger combing her hair and then motioned me to come closer. "Help me with this thing, Sweetpea."

Grandma still wore a corset. It was all hooks and laces and hard stays. Once in a while, when Grandma was tired, and her joints were all stiff, I helped her undo it. How she got into that contraption, I never could figure out.

"Grandma, why do you even wear a corset?" I struggled with a stubborn lace. "Seems like it would be hard to breathe with this old thing on." I pictured the ladies in the pictures with their arms wrapped around bedposts while their maids unlaced them.

Grandma clutched the front of the corset with one hand and her robe with the other and stepped behind the closet door to loosen the last few hooks. "At last." She flung the corset to the floor. "What we women must endure," said Grandma. "But, it would be unladylike to go without."

"Well, I'm never going to wear one," I said. "I don't even like wearing dresses all that much." Grandma's birthday surprise had been a dress and a matching coat. Blue to match my eyes, with velvet at the collar.

"I'm saving my birthday dress for when Daddy comes home," I quickly added. Didn't want Grandma to think I hated her present.

I plopped down on the vanity bench and handed her the silver-backed brush. Grandma started at the crown of my head and gently began to brush my straight-as-string hair. I counted exactly one hundred strokes. She never pulled or yanked.

"I tell you what," said Grandma after a while. "Scooter's sweeping out the store. Go ask him to please scoop you up a quart of vanilla and one of chocolate."

"Strawberry, too, Grandma. Don't forget the strawberry."

"All right, all right. Tell Scooter strawberry, too. Then you grab us a couple of bananas and one of those little jars of maraschino cherries and maybe a handful of walnuts. I'll make some chocolate sauce. You can whip the cream. We'll show Gloria what a real banana split tastes like."

I didn't have to be told twice.

Banana splits were about my favorite thing in all the world and nobody made them like Grandma. Her chocolate sauce was pure melted fudge, and she never said a thing about how much whipped cream I piled on.

Grandma got started on her fudge sauce, and I practically skipped into the store for the ice cream. When I went upstairs to get Miss Gloria, I was surprised not to find her door open. She hardly ever closed it. The only sound was "Chattanooga Choo Choo" playing on the radio. I tapped on the door. Miss Gloria didn't open it right way, and when she did, I could tell she'd been crying. Something told me I'd best not say anything about the tears on her cheeks.

"Grandma's making fudge sauce, and we're going to make banana splits. She sent me up to fetch you."

"That sounds nice, child." Miss Gloria stood stock still in the doorway. "Run along now. I'll be down real soon."

I took my time getting back to the kitchen. For a little bit, I sat on the stairs to think things over. Seeing Miss

Gloria's eyes so sad again made me glum. She was missing R.J. real bad, I figured. Her stomach probably got a big hole in it like mine did when I thought about Daddy. Good thing Grandma thought of making banana splits. The heavenly smell of chocolate brought me to my senses.

"Certainly took your time. You'd think Gloria lived in the next county." Grandma was standing by the stove, keeping an eye on the double boiler. She looked into the pot and turned the heat down low. "Now then, dear, get started on that whipped cream."

Grandma carefully dished out a scoop each of chocolate, vanilla, and strawberry into her special crystal bowls. She added a slice of banana on either side. Next came the sauce. I added the whipping cream and a sprinkling of chopped nuts. With a big old wave of her hand, Grandma put a shiny red cherry on the top.

"I think we need fanfare for this." Grandma blew a trumpet sound into her fist. I couldn't help but giggle.

"Why, those banana splits look almost too good to eat." Miss Gloria was standing in the doorway. She looked newly scrubbed and had pinned her hair back over her ears. Not a tear in sight.

"You're just in time," I said. "The ice cream will be just

slushy enough and the sauce will be hard and cold like frozen fudge. You're in for a real treat!"

No one said a word for several minutes. Just a lot of slurping sounds — mostly from me — and the clunk of spoons against the bowls. We were busy concentrating on our ice cream.

"That was lovely. Can't say that I've ever had a banana split quite like that." Miss Gloria let out a long satisfied kind of sigh.

"What special treat did your grandma make for you?" I asked.

"Pecan pie," said Miss Gloria. "My grandmother was from Louisiana. Her pecan pie would just about melt in your mouth. I'll make you one soon." Her voice dropped and got all choked up, like she had a lump in her throat.

I looked at Grandma, and she gave her head a shake that said, "Let me handle this."

"Are you all right, Gloria?" said Grandma. "A little homesickness maybe?" She reached across the table for Miss Gloria's hand. "Annie and I are good listeners, if you'd like to talk a spell."

Miss Gloria's elbows were resting on the table. Her head was cradled in her left hand. "I don't want to burden you." It seemed like she was trying extra hard not to burst into tears.

"I'm not sure what I'm homesick for, exactly. Surely not the humidity." She looked up and managed a smile that was gone in a flash. "My folks are both gone. Most of those I loved back home are gone, too. Nothing much to miss about Georgia. Why, you even have dogwood." There was a flicker of a smile again.

Grandma and I were real quiet. Was she thinking what I was? That because of Uncle Billy and that nasty Ben Jackson and the cross burning, Miss Gloria was about to pack up and leave?

"I'd like to hear more about your life in Georgia," Grandma said. "You're from Athens, right? I don't know much about the South. My late husband's people were from Texas, but I guess that's not exactly the South."

Grandma put on the tea kettle and bustled around the kitchen. And not a word about me getting ready for bed. She got out her Sunday china cups and we took our tea into the living room.

"Let's have us an evening of girl talk," Grandma said after we had settled on the sofa.

For the rest of the evening Miss Gloria painted us a real

nice picture of growing up in the South. I liked her stories about catching fireflies in old fruit jars. She said in the summer the nights were so hot straight through midnight that most people stayed out on their porches until early morning. I found out her parents had both been teachers. Grandma asked her tons of questions about Georgia gardens, and I wanted to know more about those horses she rode. We were listening so hard that at first we didn't hear the knocking at the front door.

Grandma finally excused herself and got up to go answer it. "Who in the world could that be? It's already past nine."

I couldn't make out who was at the door. Grandma's voice was low and all I could hear was a lot of mumbling. Then Grandma let out a shriek. Miss Gloria and I jumped up at the same time and scurried into the hall to the front door. Grandma was slumped against the hallstand where we kept our galoshes and umbrellas. She was clutching a telegram. My heart dropped to my shoes. I knew what telegrams meant: they brought the very worst kind of news.

Miss Gloria put her arm around Grandma and helped her sit down on the hall seat.

"Lord have mercy! I hope it isn't about Mr. Eddie."

"It is," said Grandma. "Oh, but it is."

I couldn't help myself. Right then and there I started to howl.

Grandma reached out and patted my head. "No, sweetheart, don't cry. The telegram's from the Red Cross. They've located your daddy. In France. Can you imagine?"

Then we all started to cry. Even Miss Gloria. But these were tears of pure joy.

Chapter 14

For the next few days, I went around feeling all out of sorts. Seemed like I spent hours on gobs of homework. Miss Gloria was real sweet. She helped me with my numbers when I got stuck. It was hard to concentrate, though. I was mostly thinking about Daddy coming home and worrying about Uncle Billy. Half the time I didn't know whether to laugh or cry. I hated to call him out on a Saturday, but I needed to talk to Mr. Truman. He'd help me sort things out.

"I sure hope you don't think I'm an awful pest, bringing you out to Walla Walla on a day you could be doing something really swell, but here's the thing, my daddy's been found, and I just had to tell you." Well, before I could get out anything more, the President lit up like a Christmas tree, and a big grin spread clear across his face.

"Aw, you knew already." I for sure could've hugged him, but I figured a person just didn't walk up to President Truman and give him a big old bear hug.

"Now, Annie Leigh, I can't take all the credit. You get the lion's share of that. Why, with the energy from all those wishes alone and all that love, not to mention those prayers of yours, your daddy was bound to turn up." Mr. Truman wrinkled the space between his eyebrows. "But why the long face?"

"Grandma's making all kinds of plans one minute and then telling me not to get my hopes up too high the next. It's like too much talk about Daddy will jinx it. I don't know what to think. Mama finally got herself a phone in her new place, and I've called her a dozen times. Grandma didn't say one word about how much it cost. I mean, there's all kinds of things to do. Everybody's going around in circles."

Mr. Truman and I were sitting out in the lawn swing, and he gave it two or three shoves before he answered me. We just sat quietly and let it swing for such a long while that I looked over to see if maybe he'd dropped off for a quick snooze. He was wide awake. The look on his face told me he was thinking real hard about what I'd said.

"You just go right ahead and believe your daddy is coming home, Annie Leigh. Folks are just a little shy about accepting good news when they've been grieving for so long. It's kind of like being on a carousel. When it suddenly stops unexpectedly, you walk around all wobbly until you get your balance again."

I took in a big breath. I had a lot to think about. But wouldn't you know, Grandma took that very moment to stick her head out the back door.

"Stop dawdling, Annie Leigh; you promised to help Scooter shelve canned goods this morning."

I had to ask Mr. Truman one more truly important question before I went in the store. "What should I do about Billy?" I asked him. "If he knew Daddy'd been found, he might feel better about lots of stuff." But the president just put his finger to his lips, tipped his hat, and was gone.

Maybe Scooter could help. If I could just see Uncle Billy without that Ben Jackson hiding in the shrubbery, I might get somewhere.

Scooter was working in the soup aisle, dusting each can

like it was a piece of good china. "Hey there, Annie," he said. "Doggone it if that isn't good news about your daddy. Your Grandma told me about the telegram."

"We don't know too much yet." I didn't want to talk about Daddy and get all clammy and nervous. Besides, it was Billy I needed to talk about.

Scooter pushed a box of soup in my direction and pointed at the shelf next to me. "Start stacking, kiddo, or we'll be here all day."

"I wish Billy would straighten up. Grandma thinks it's the war that changed him."

"Could be. I reckon your uncle saw some things no man ought to witness in his lifetime."

"Like what?" I'd never really thought much about what Billy had done in the war.

"Your Uncle Billy was a plain old foot soldier, not a fly boy like your daddy. He spent most of his time in the war freezing to death in a cold foxhole, watching all his best buddies die around him. Must weigh heavy on a fellow knowing he made it home alive but none of the others did."

"I don't know what you're talking about."

"Billy was the only man left in his platoon who made it," Scooter said matter-of-factly.

"You mean, he was the only one who came home?" I got goose bumps thinking about what Billy must have seen. "Not even one other fellow lived?"

"Nope." Scooter shook his head and studied a can of tomato soup for a good long while. "I'm not sure talking about the war is fit conversation for a girl."

"Girls were in the war, too," I said. "If they were in the army, they were WACS. And if I'd been old enough, I'd have signed up real fast."

"That so!" Scooter let out a little coughing sound and rolled his eyes. "Now that would have been something. The Germans wouldn't have known what hit 'em with you around."

"I'm serious, Scooter. I need your help to straighten Billy out. He's breaking Grandma's heart with all his carrying on."

Scooter didn't say anything for a while. He just kept polishing the same can of tomato soup.

"You're going to rub that label right off the can." I figured he knew a whole lot about Uncle Billy that he wasn't saying. "You and Billy used to be friends. How come you don't run around together anymore?"

"Like I told you before, he don't have much time for his old pals, especially a gimp like me."

That was the first time Scooter had ever mentioned his bum foot. As long as I'd known him, he'd always walked with a kind of skip and a shuffle. The story was he'd hurt his foot in a threshing machine years before. Guess kids had teased him all through school, and Uncle Billy had always stood up for him. Things sure had changed.

"Now that Daddy's coming home, I have some serious things to discuss with Billy," I said. "But first he has to apologize to Grandma and Miss Gloria."

"He'll come around with your grandma, though I can't figure out what got him into such a state about Miss Washington. She's a real nice lady, and I don't remember your Uncle Billy ever having anything against a Negro before."

"Maybe you could talk to him, Scooter. He only pops in and out of here to cause a fuss, and there's no talking to him."

"First you got to promise me something." Scooter slapped his hand over his heart. "I'll see what I can find out, but you got to promise me you won't go poking around on your own."

I put my hand over my heart and held up three fingers. "Promise. Scout's honor." Scooter looked solemn as a preacher.

I didn't like lying, but it was a promise I knew I couldn't keep.

"Now then," said Scooter. "Think you can speed it up a mite? You haven't shelved but three cans in the last five minutes."

Seemed to me shelving cans was the last thing I needed to be doing. Scooter finally gave up on me. "You're slower'n molasses in January. Go on, git."

I left Scooter mumbling to himself while he lined up the cans I'd just shelved. Never knew a fellow to be such a fussbudget.

Thing was, I just had to talk to Billy myself, especially now that I knew he'd lost all his friends in the war. But I wasn't sure how to do that without lying to Grandma, too. She'd have seven kinds of fits knowing I was wandering around town by myself, and she most definitely wouldn't want me down at Halverson's Feed and Fuel. But that was the only place I knew to look. If Billy wasn't there, Mr. Halverson could most likely tell me where to find him.

It was nearly lunch, and not a soul was in the kitchen, but the whole place smelled of spice cake. Grandma was in the little office talking on the phone. She clearly hadn't been doing any baking. It had to be Miss Gloria. Ever since we heard about Daddy, she'd been baking like it was Christmas. Sure enough, right in the middle of the table was a big three-layer cake with burnt sugar frosting. I cut myself a big piece and wrapped it in a hanky. It would have to do for lunch.

"Going to the library," I yelled in to Grandma. Before she could say a word, I was out the back door.

Halverson's was a lot farther away then I remembered. It was blocks and blocks past the library. I promised myself I'd stop in on my way home and check out a book. That way I hadn't really and truly lied to Grandma.

By the time I got to the feed store, I had a blister on my heel and was dying of thirst. Nibbling on the cake the whole way had made my mouth dry as dust.

"Well, lookee here," said Mr. Halverson. "It's Hattie Howard's little Annie. What can I do for you, Missy?"

"Need a drink," I croaked. Mr. Halverson pointed to

the back of the store. A big square sink stood near the rack of shovels. I was tempted to stick my head under the faucet and lap up the water like a dog, but I scooped some water in my hand instead. Someone in the corner was having himself a good laugh. The sound of it sent a chill right up my spine.

"Well, if it isn't Little Miss Big Mouth." Ben Jackson was leaning up against a stack of boxes, chewing on a toothpick. "Hallie, here's one young lady far too big for her britches."

"I'm looking for my Uncle Billy," I said. "I've got something awful important to tell him."

Mr. Halverson folded his arms and looked straight at me across the counter. "Can't say as I know where Billy is." He nodded his head at Ben Jackson. I was sure they were sending each other all kinds of eye signals.

For the life of me, I couldn't figure out why Mr. Halverson put up with such trash.

"Pretty soon my daddy's coming home, and Billy needs to make things right with Grandma."

"Your daddy ain't never comin' home, Missy." Ben Jackson dug around in his pocket before he put a whole plug of tobacco in his cheek.

"Is so! We got a telegram."

"Is that a fact?" Ben said. "Now that's the kind of news your Uncle Billy's going to be real happy to hear. *Real* happy."

What a mean old cuss! The meanness was just dribbling out of his mouth, along with the tobacco juice. Of course Billy would be happy to see Daddy. That Ben Jackson wasn't just a rotten apple, he was a big dope to boot!

"You don't know nuthin' about it, Ben, so keep your mouth shut," Mr. Halverson said. He waved his hand at me. "Run along now, Annie. If I see Billy, I'll give him your news."

I was half way down the block when a car pulled up beside me. "Hey, little girl. Want a ride?"

A chill cold as ice raced up my spine. I just kept right on walking. Ben Jackson followed close behind all the way to the library. My heart was beating so hard and fast I was sure it was going to stick to my throat.

I flew up the library steps two at a time, whirled my way through the revolving door, and didn't slow down until I'd reached a back room full of old dusty books. I slumped to the floor in a heap, trying to catch my breath.

That old knucklehead Ben Jackson wasn't going to scare me. I wouldn't let him.

The sound of footsteps made me jump. I pulled a book off the shelf right in front of me and pretended I was studying something real important. A pair of giant bug eyes jumped right off the page and stared back at me. Ugh!

"Well, I'll be," said a familiar voice. "So this is how you spend your Saturday afternoons. Lookin' at plug ugly bugs." Billy let out a whoop so loud a librarian poked her head in the door and hushed him.

"How'd you know where I was?"

"A little bird told me." Billy reached over and tugged at a strand of my hair. "Now let's get out of here so we can have us a talk."

For just the tiniest second, Billy seemed like his old self again. I sure missed that Billy.

"Talk to Grandma," I said. "You gotta say you're sorry."

Billy took my arm and marched me right back out to the library steps and onto the bus bench on the corner. "Listen, twerp. You got to stop poking into other people's business."

"What happens to Grandma is my business, and you've

no right to be so mean to Miss Gloria. She's my friend, and she's real nice to Grandma."

Billy changed the subject. "So your dad's comin' home after all." He wasn't smiling anymore. "Tell me about the telegram."

He pulled a pack of cigarettes out of his pocket and lit one. I filled him in on what I knew, but there wasn't much to tell.

"Now don't that beat all," he said, blowing smoke in my direction.

"Come on home and talk to Grandma. She's been on the phone all day about Daddy." I batted at the smoke. "And you better not let Grandma see you smoking."

"Your grandma don't want me around." Billy took a big drag on his cigarette. "And, anyways, I don't figure your grandma's house is big enough for both me and your Miss Gloria." He shook his head and flicked his cigarette out into the street.

I reached over and put my hand on Billy's. "Scooter says you saw bad things in the war."

Billy pulled away and jammed his hands into his jacket pockets. "Yeah, well. What does he know about anything?"

"I know you came back all different." I scooted closer to Billy and stuck my arm through his. "You used to be an awful pest, but I'd give anything to have that Uncle Billy back instead of this mean one."

"Well, there's a lot of things I'd like, too," said Billy. "I'd like the world to make sense. I'd like certain people to know their place. I'd like a little respect." Billy pulled my arm out of his and jumped up. "Go on home now. You shouldn't be out wandering the streets."

Billy wanted everyone to think he was real tough. He wasn't. I thought about what Scooter had told me. Losing all kinds of friends would make me real sad too, and watching them die . . . well, I couldn't imagine how bad that would feel. But it might make me madder than a wet hen. So mad I might want to scratch a few eyes out, or maybe slap somebody silly. Miss Gloria was right. Uncle Billy had something eating at him that was mighty powerful.

"You got to promise to make things right with Grandma before Daddy gets home," I said. Then I moved closer and put my hand on his arm. Before he could move aside, I stood on my tiptoes to kiss him on the cheek. He leaned toward me, but then he quickly turned away and started across the street.

"Go on, kid," he said over his shoulder. "Go on home."

"Billy, wait!" Right there in the middle of the street, in front of the library, I threw my arms around Billy and hugged him as tight as I could.

"Come on home, Billy," I whispered.

I swear he hugged me back for a full minute before he pushed me away.

"Now, git!" He tried to sound tough, but his voice cracked, and he had to swallow hard. "Leave me be."

Seemed to me that was the last thing Billy really wanted. Even with all the hateful things he'd done and said, I wasn't going to leave him be. Billy Howard seemed like about the loneliest soul I knew.

Chapter 15

By the time I got home, it was way past lunch. No one was in the kitchen, so I walked in the back door and tiptoed up to my room. Turned out, Miss Gloria was right where she'd been when I'd left. Whew! She hadn't even noticed I'd been gone.

After school a few days later, Miss Gloria and I were sitting in the little office together. She was helping me with my speech for the Armistice Day contest at school. I was writing about Daddy and what a brave pilot he was.

"There's a lot of fine words in here, child," she said. "But I'm not sure I hear your sweet voice behind them." She looked at me over her glasses. "What is it? You've been chewing on something for days. Something happened last Saturday, didn't it?"

"How do you know?"

"I saw you sneak in right after lunch and drag yourself upstairs. You've been a million miles away ever since." Miss Gloria was smiling, but I knew she was dead serious.

Dang! I hadn't gotten away with anything.

"I saw Billy." I wouldn't have dared tell Grandma what happened, but I told Miss Gloria everything. She listened quietly until I finished.

"Just hoping your uncle will be the person you want him to be won't make it so," she said sadly. "No matter how much you want it to be true."

I didn't want Miss Gloria to think I'd forgotten that Billy had acted like a skunk. Maybe standing up for him made me sound like a bad friend.

"I've been so mad at him, Miss Gloria, but you should have seen him. Billy was just the saddest thing. I think he's real mixed-up, and I bet he's sorry about everything. He just doesn't know how to tell us."

"I know how badly you want your Uncle Billy to be the same person he was before the war, but he has to find his own way back. I declare, child, you can't go poking around this city alone. Especially with that ugly Ben Jackson prowling about like an old polecat." Miss Gloria shuffled the papers in her lap.

"Now then, let's get back to your speech." She pushed her glasses back up on her nose.

"I've been thinking," I said. "There's a lot of important things to tell about Daddy, but maybe I'll put in some things about Uncle Billy, too."

"Good idea. Sometimes putting things down on paper helps you understand a person's intentions more clearly." Miss Gloria handed me a fresh piece of paper and a newly sharpened pencil. "Words can be a mighty force for healing. A person just has to read Mr. Lincoln to know that."

I pored over those words until I thought my eyes would cross. When Miss Gloria thought I was ready, she had me stand at one end of the dining room table, and she sat at the other. I read what I'd written about a thousand times.

"Practicing is hard work," I whined.

"Let's try something," said Miss Gloria. "Just sit down and tell it to me like we were two friends over a cup of tea."

And that's just what we did. Miss Gloria made a pot of tea, and we sat and talked 'til dark. I did go on. Didn't know I had so much to say inside me.

Miss Gloria let out a big sigh. "Now that was nice. Real natural. That's your speech!" She gave my head a pat. "And now it's dinnertime, and your grandma will be in from the store soon. Let's go start some potatoes."

No one could get a word in edgewise over dinner. I just kept rattling on. Miss Gloria told Grandma what I'd written was real fine, and I was real proud.

My fine speech didn't get me out of washing the dinner dishes, but around eight o'clock Grandma called me into the living room. She'd put up the ironing board in front of the bay window.

"Now, imagine that's your podium," she said. "Let me hear what you and Gloria have been going on about."

For the next several minutes I looked out at Grandma and said the words that were closest to my heart. When I'd finished, Grandma and Miss Gloria were real quiet. Then they were both talking at once.

"Oh, that's sure to be a winner," said Miss Gloria.

"My, oh, my," said Grandma. "That was truly wonderful. Inspiring. That part about how most folks at home thought sacrifice was going without sugar and butter, but that men like your daddy and your uncle had given up a whole lot more, sometimes their lives — why, that gave me goose bumps." She put her arm around me and pulled me close. "Wherever did that come from?"

"I've been thinking about it ever since I had a talk with Scooter about Uncle Billy. Made me remember how it used to bother me when customers complained all the time about no butter and no coffee. And there was Daddy flying dangerous missions and Uncle Billy lying in the mud, with maybe no dry socks, and bullets flying everywhere."

Grandma pulled me in closer for a hug. "My stars, Sweetpea, when did you get to be so grown-up?"

"This calls for a special treat!" Miss Gloria said and disappeared into the kitchen. She returned with a bowl piled high with popcorn and a plate of pumpkin cookies left over from Halloween. "There's hot cider simmering in the kitchen, too."

When Miss Gloria went back for the cider, I moved over to the sofa. Grandma snuggled up right beside me and gave me a tap on my nose.

"It's time we got you those glasses," she said. "And don't wrinkle up your face at me! You squinted every time you peeked at your notes."

Miss Gloria talked Grandma into letting me buy frames with a little rhinestone in each corner so at least I didn't look like a dope wearing them. When I turned a certain way, a miniature rainbow sparkled in the corner of my eye. Those glasses must have brought me luck, because the day we presented our speeches in class, mine was chosen as one of the five finalists. In less than two weeks, on the evening of November 11, 1946, I would stand up before the entire school and a whole mess of parents and talk about why Daddy and Uncle Billy were heroes.

The rest of the day my two feet were miles above the floor. Grandma would be so proud of me! Miss Gloria, too. It wasn't likely Daddy could get home in time to hear my speech, but I hoped Uncle Billy would feel a lot better about things once he heard it.

My feet didn't touch solid ground until the final bell rang and I was down the steps and on my way home. An icy wind had whipped up, so I buttoned my coat all the way up to my neck and put my hands over my ears to keep the cold out. I was halfway across the playground before I realized Uncle Billy was standing by the bus bench at the corner.

"Billy," I yelled. "Wait up! I got something to tell you."

He just stood there with a dumb look on his face.

"Whoa, Annie. I'm not going anywhere. I was waiting for you."

"What are you doing here?"

"You ain't too big to be walked home, are you?" Billy pulled up the collar on his moth-eaten army jacket. "Dadblast it, that wind's cold. Where are your mittens?"

"I'm eleven. Mittens are for babies." Billy sure had a way of taking a person's wind out of their sails.

"Here, put these on." Billy pulled a pair of dark brown gloves out of his jacket pocket and waved them in my face. "No back-talk now. You oughta be wearing a hat or ear-muffs."

What in tarnation had gotten into him? "You're awful bossy today," I said. "But bossy sure is better than mean."

"You need someone to tell you what to do. Ma lets you run wild. That Miss Gloria teaching you bad habits?"

"No! She helps me with my homework. She figured out I needed glasses. She knows about a lot of things." I threw his gloves on the ground and walked ahead.

"If you're going to say ugly things about Miss Gloria, I'm going on along home by my very own self. I had something important to tell you. You don't even care."

"Aww, come on back, Missy. I'll buy you a hot chocolate. In a minute your nose is going to freeze and drop off." He bent over and picked up his gloves. "Go on now," he said, giving my hair a good yank. "Put these back on, twerp."

I gave him a swat back, and we had ourselves a play fight all the way to Mr. Peterson's Drug Store.

An old man came around the corner and shook his cane at Billy. "That's no way to treat your little sister, young man."

That got us to laughing real hard. Folks were always mistaking Billy for my big brother. And I used to wish he was.

The drugstore was nearly empty, but Billy still picked out a booth way in the back. He got me hot cocoa with extra whipped cream, and a coffee for himself. Before he could get a word out, I started telling Billy about the contest at school.

"It's for Armistice Day," I said. "My speech was chosen in my class, so I get to give it in front of the whole school. You got to promise you'll come, Billy."

"Maybe." Billy was awful fidgety. He kept digging at

the sugar and spooning it back into the bowl. He hadn't touched his coffee.

"I saw your grandma this afternoon," he said finally.

"Did you tell her you were real sorry?"

"Ma and I had us a nice long talk, mostly about your daddy."

"What'd she say? And when's he coming home exactly? When I ask her, she just tells me everything's fine, but I want to know when I'll get to see Daddy again."

"Looks like he'll be home around Thanksgiving." Billy pushed his coffee cup aside and leaned across the table. "You know what amnesia is, Annie Leigh?"

"It's when a person can't remember his name or his wife and kids and stuff." What in the world were we talking about that for? "I saw a movie once where this man had two wives because he couldn't remember he had the first one."

Billy smiled a nice smile. It was good to see it on his face. "Well, the reason your daddy's been missing for so long is he had amnesia."

"That's why he's in France and not where he was supposed to be?"

"Something like that," said Billy. "But he's not in

France anymore. He's in some hospital back East. Has to be checked out by army doctors before he can come home."

"Is he still sick?"

"Your daddy's not sick. Amnesia's not like having the measles or chicken pox, and anyway he doesn't have amnesia anymore."

"I know that." Boy! Billy could get a person worked up, even when he was trying to be nice. "I'm not that dumb. You get amnesia from a bump on the head or something like that."

"As far as anyone can tell, your daddy most likely bailed out of a plane just inside Italy." Billy pulled out a cigarette and lit it. I made a face and he blew a few smoke rings in my direction.

"After that, the details are a little patchy, but he must have had a pretty good conk on the head, 'cause he plumb forgot who he was. Everything got crazy at the end of the war, but somehow he ended up in a French hospital."

Billy hesitated. "Ma's been waiting for the right time to tell you all this, but I figured, no time like the present."

I could tell he was poking around in his head for the right words to give me some bad news.

"Your daddy's lost his sight," he said. Billy hadn't come to walk me home 'cause he was turning over a new leaf. He was just back to being mean.

"That's not true! You know it isn't! You're a liar." I felt my eyes begin to sting. "If Daddy couldn't see, Grandma would have told me already. You're just being ugly again."

I worked hard at fighting off tears. But soon they were falling fast and hot on my cheeks. I kicked Billy hard under the table. He didn't say anything. Just passed me a napkin. My hands stayed frozen in my lap, and I kept on crying, right into my cocoa.

"Daddy's not blind. You're just making that up. He just forgot who he was for a time. Soon he'll be home, and we'll do all the things I've planned."

"C'mon, Annie," said Billy. "Let me walk you back home."

He slid out of the booth and took my arm. I jerked it back. "Leave me alone. I can walk home by myself." I began to pound Billy with my fists. "I hate you, Billy Howard! I hate you!"

Mr. Peterson started to walk over to us, but Billy waved him off. I turned away and scooted closer to the wall. When I looked up, Billy was gone. At that moment, I felt like I could throw a big fit right there in the middle of the drugstore. I sincerely hoped Mr. Truman was busy with a big cabinet meeting. I sure didn't want him to see the truly ugly side of Annie Leigh Howard.

Mr. Peterson put a fresh cup of hot cocoa in front of me. But my bones felt all cold. A chill went right down my spine, through my itchy wool socks, and settled in my toes. No amount of cocoa was ever going to make me warm again.

Chapter 16

I was quiet all through dinner, pushing my peas around and making little mountains out of my mashed potatoes. Grandma usually scolded me for messing with my vegetables, but tonight she just kept asking me to say something.

Blindness. I didn't want to talk about it. After I'd come home from the drugstore, Grandma had sat me down for another one of our heart-to-hearts. She told me straight out that Uncle Billy hadn't lied, that my daddy really was blind. I didn't tell her I'd yelled at Billy right in front of Mr. Peterson and just about the whole of Walla Walla. Grandma also told me that Mama had taken the train back East to be with Daddy. Without me.

"Your mama and daddy need some time alone together." Grandma was trying to put the best face on everything, but she just ended up sounding wretched. The house was going to sink into the creek from so much sadness.

"What if Daddy doesn't remember me? If he can't see me, how will he know who I am?" I said. "Do you think maybe he stayed lost 'cause he didn't want to be found?"

Grandma didn't have an answer for that. She just held onto me real tight and whispered, "Everything's going to be fine," over and over in my ear.

My insides had been on a roller coaster ride ever since yesterday, and they were still rolling. Mama must have known how bad I wanted to be with her when she saw Daddy. Why, I would've run alongside a train if it led me to his hospital bed. Probably, Mama was so excited to see Daddy that she got on the first train she could. Hope she took her blue dress, the one Daddy bought her just before he left. She looks like a movie star in it. Then I remembered: Daddy wouldn't be able to see her.

Later, when I was upstairs and supposed to be asleep, I tossed and turned and wrestled with the covers. I could hear Grandma moving around downstairs. She was restless, too. Miss Gloria stuck her head in the door.

"Can't sleep?" She straightened the blankets and sat

down on the edge of the bed. "Why don't I keep the radio on and my door open until you fall asleep." And she jumped up like that was the best idea ever and was across the hall and back in a flash. "Fibber McGee and Molly" was about to start.

"I'll sit with you a while," said Miss Gloria, "but only until Fibber opens up his closet."

"Mama and Daddy and I used to listen together every Tuesday night. We'd sit and wait 'til Molly said, ''Tain't funny, McGee,' and then yell it back to the radio and laugh 'til our sides hurt."

"You'll do that again, child. Real soon."

I closed my eyes and held my palms against my lids. A blind person must get scared of all that dark. With my eyes shut tight, I reached up to find Miss Gloria's face.

"If I were blind, I'd have to see you with my hands." I felt her skin, all buttery smooth and soft. Then I opened my eyes. "It's much better this way."

Miss Gloria reached over and smoothed back my hair. "Soon your daddy will be home and you'll have to show him some of that famous Annie Leigh Howard grit. It can be a hard life without your sight. But just being home with you all — you and your grandma and your mama, why, that will make your daddy's life as sweet as anyone could hope for. Don't forget that." Miss Gloria leaned over and tucked the covers around me and gave me a kiss on the cheek.

And then we heard all that junk crash out of Fibber McGee's closet. "'Tain't funny, McGee," I whispered. And I was asleep before Miss Gloria could whisper it back.

The next morning there wasn't a soul in the kitchen. The shade on the back door was still down, and the fire in the stove had gone cold. Grandma always stoked it before she went to bed, so there'd be a few embers to light the next morning.

Funny, no coffee on to boil. No oatmeal, either. Grandma never slept past six, and it was already seven. I peeked inside her room. She was making little soft hooting sounds in her sleep. If I was going to get to school on time, I'd have to be the cook. It was too late for cereal, so I helped myself to one of the day-old doughnuts Grandma had in the breadbox. I ate off all the sprinkles and licked at the frosting. My throat felt full of little knives.

Things didn't get much better as the week went on. Every morning at the beginning of class, Miss Dibble in- sisted we all give our speeches. I kept stumbling through mine. By the end of the week, the words seemed to catch in my throat.

"Concentrate," Miss Dibble kept repeating. "Think about the meaning of the words."

That was the trouble. I was thinking too much, trying to picture what it would be like when Daddy came home. My fine words weren't going to help him see, or make Uncle Billy any happier. All this time I'd been missing Daddy like crazy, and now that he was really and truly coming home, I wasn't sure what to do next. I knew better than to expect Mama would bring Daddy to Walla Walla in time for my speech, but I kept hoping that somehow that wish would come true.

By the afternoon of the contest, a terrible sadness had come over me. When I came home from school, the bottom of my stomach must have been around my shoes.

Miss Gloria and Grandma fussed over me something terrible. Miss Gloria rolled my hair in rags the minute I walked in the door. She wanted it to fluff out all curly for the competition. Grandma got me a Shirley Temple bow for the curls and made a big thing about pressing my birthday dress. She usually hated ironing.

Scooter even picked us up in his uncle Orville's big

shiny Buick and drove us the two blocks to school. Grandma protested and said it was a waste of gasoline, but she had a silly jack-o'-lantern smile on her face the whole ride.

Once we got inside the auditorium, a few butterflies danced around in my stomach. Miss Dibble waved at me and had me follow her to the stage where the others were already seated.

I looked out at the crowd, searching for Billy. He wasn't there. Probably wasn't coming. Maybe I was right all along. Maybe he was just pure hateful. I had yelled at him and called him a liar. Those words had burst out of my mouth so fast there was no time to take them back. Billy probably didn't care about my old speech anyway.

I shifted in my chair. How could a room that was big enough to hold half the town feel like the furnace was on full blast? My petticoat was stuck to the back of my legs. I looked out over the stage lights. Still no Billy, but there was Grandma in the front row, and Miss Gloria right next to her. Couldn't help but wish Mama and Daddy could be there, too.

I had the worst luck to be last. It seemed ages before my name was called. By then, my curls had drooped, and my collar was a soggy mess. Plus the butterflies in my stomach had multiplied.

"Ladies and gentlemen," I began. My voice squeaked and the microphone groaned. The butterflies in my stomach started a game of hopscotch. I took a quick glance at the audience. Sure enough, there was Mr. Truman way in the back. I might have missed him, but he had on that white suit of his. He gave me the go-ahead sign, and I began again.

Wouldn't you know it, as soon as I opened my mouth, one of the big back doors swung open. It was Scooter, and Billy was with him. A rustle of whispers went through the audience. I kept going, but now I spoke directly to Billy.

"When it came to fighting the war, kids didn't get much of a say. We bought lots of war bonds and pulled our wagons around the neighborhoods collecting tin cans and old newspapers. We weren't asked to do anything all that special. Eating tons of Spam and dry toast and growing Victory gardens wasn't much of a sacrifice. Not anything like what our soldiers had to give up. The war may be over now, but it hasn't ended for everyone. I'm only a kid, but I hope you'll listen to what I have to say."

All of a sudden I felt light as air. Something had taken

hold and pulled that awful sadness right out of me. I didn't have to think about the words this time. They just came, smooth as silk. People needed to remember that soldiers like Daddy and Uncle Billy had lost a lot. It was bad enough that Daddy had lost his sight, but some soldiers like Uncle Billy lost all of their friends and came back with empty hearts. My voice had a funny flutter in it by the end, but the butterflies were long gone. I didn't even need to look at my notes.

"On this Armistice Day we remember those who died. But tomorrow when you pour a cup of coffee or cover your toast in butter, think about those boys who came back. After fighting a war, it has to be hard to come home and just pick up where you left off. Think of all those soldiers who may look like they are doing just swell, but need help putting all the pieces back together. Once they are mended, that's when we can say the war is truly over."

The room had grown real quiet. Not a sound. Then a little ripple of applause started in the back of the auditorium. By the time it got to the front, it seemed like the whole audience was clapping. My legs started to shake, and I felt light-headed.

Billy had disappeared by then, but I knew he'd heard

everything. Down in front of me, Grandma and Miss Gloria were on their feet clapping as hard as they could. I gave them a wave and wobbled back to my chair.

Miss Dibble stepped up to the microphone. She had a few words to say herself, and she went on in that funny way she had, like someone was pinching her nose. And then she went on some more. She was marking time until the judges made their decision. The people in the audience were making little rustling noises and waving their programs to cool off. A few of them were yawning. When Miss Dibble finally got to the winner, I was barely listening.

"And first prize goes to . . . Annie Leigh Howard."

I sat there unable to move. Was everyone looking at me? Had Miss Dibble just said my name?

I looked over at her, and she looked puzzled. She waggled her head at me to come forward. I looked down at Grandma and she was waggling her head as well. I got up like a sleepwalker. Had I really won?

Miss Dibble handed me a certificate and then placed a ribbon around my neck. It held a gold medallion that read "First Prize."

Grandma met me at the bottom of the stairs and hugged me until I could hardly breathe.

"That was a real good speech, Annie Leigh," said Scooter. He leaned down to give me a hug. "Just wanted you to know," he whispered, "your Uncle Billy heard every word. Every word."

Before I could ask him where Billy had gone, Scooter was off in the crowd, and Grandma and Miss Gloria were both talking at once. I gave a quick look for Mr. Truman, but I expect he slipped out before those Secret Service fellows got all in a snit.

Since Grandma's hip was acting up, she planned to ask Scooter for a ride home. Miss Gloria and I decided to walk. She was ready to get some air after the stuffy auditorium, and that was fine with me. We could hardly get out the door for people stopping to congratulate me.

"Now, don't you go and get a swelled head." Miss Gloria gave what was left of my curls a yank. I was dizzy with joy. By the time we got home, we had laughed ourselves silly.

"That teacher of yours has the most peculiar way with words," said Miss Gloria. "For the longest time I thought she was saying 'otters' instead of 'orators.'"

I sucked in my cheeks and made sour pickle lips. "Lahdies and Jauntelmen," I began.

We collapsed on the back steps, shrieking with laughter. Grabbing for the screen door, I lost my balance and dropped the house key. We both struggled to find it in the dark. Grandma would be unhappy at a lost key.

"Oh, child, you have that Miss Dibble right down to her shoes. You have a gift." Her voice turned more solemn. "But, really Annie, you shouldn't make fun." She couldn't finish, and we started to laugh all over again. Miss Gloria got down on her knees to help me find the key.

"Oh, my, I do believe I've ruined my last pair of silk stockings." She pointed at a smudge of mud on my new coat. "That won't do, either."

Everything seemed funny, and it felt good to laugh. Finally we gave up the search and sat down on the steps to wait for Grandma. She must have gotten caught up talking with somebody or other at the school.

"Hush," Miss Gloria said suddenly and pulled me closer. "Do you hear something? See something down by the creek?"

Big dark shapes were moving across the lawn. I heard someone laugh. My legs started to tremble. Miss Gloria yanked me up and moved me toward the back porch. It was Ben Jackson, swaggering around the yard like he owned the place.

"Lookee here, fellows. We got ourselves some bait." He moved closer and made like he was going to grab me.

Miss Gloria put her arm around my waist and held tight.

"Now, you have no business with this child," she said. "Leave her be and move on before Missus Howard gets home."

"We're shakin' in our boots, ain't we, boys?"

The boys turned out to be Mr. Halverson's son Jeb, and a tall pock-marked guy I'd seen around who everyone called Tater. Most folks knew Jeb. He'd fallen off a horse when he was nine and never been right in the head since. Folks also knew Jeb would do about anything if you bought him enough candy.

Ben Jackson stomped the toe of his boot on the bottom step. "Where's that Uncle Billy of yours? We got things to talk about."

"How'd I know?" I said. "He doesn't live here anymore." What had Billy gone and done to get these boys riled up?

"Stop pestering this child," said Miss Gloria. "How is she supposed to know where her uncle is?"

"Now, you be quiet," said Ben Jackson. "As soon as we've finished with Billy, we've got some business with you."

"Yeah, business with you," Jeb repeated. "Business with you."

"Hey," called a voice over by the garage. It was Billy. "What are you all doing here?"

Uncle Billy took his time coming up the back walk. A big bulky package was stuck under his arm. "This is for you, Annie Leigh. Why aren't you inside? And where's Ma?"

I mumbled something about the lost key but didn't open his package. I needed to keep my wits about me in case those ol' boys were about to pull a fast one.

Ben, Tater, and Jeb circled around Billy, talking in low, angry voices. I couldn't make out what they were saying, but they sounded real mad.

Miss Gloria pushed me inside the back porch and latched the screen door. "Where in the world is your Grandma and that Scooter? I don't like the feel of this one bit."

Then Ben Jackson punched Billy in the stomach, and before Billy could get his balance, Ben pushed him real hard. Jeb grabbed his arm. They were pretty near in the creek. Something flashed. A knife? Tater had a knife! I flipped the latch and was out the door before Miss Gloria could stop me.

"Billy," I yelled, "he's got a knife!" I threw myself at Tater's knees, and he swatted me off like an old fly. Miss Gloria was at the bottom of the steps yelling. She had a carpet sweeper in her hands and was ready to give those nasty bullies a good thrashing.

Billy was trying to fight off the three boys, but he was losing. I flew at Ben Jackson. He pushed me away. I stumbled around trying to get my balance and ended up in the creek. The cold took my breath away. I flapped my arms around to keep from going under, but the mossy rocks were too slippery. All I got for my trouble was a whole mouth full of creek water. I spit and sputtered my way back onto the grass like a wet cat.

For a minute everything was in slow motion. I lay on the grass and watched Tater grab Billy by the neck. It looked like Ben Jackson and Miss Gloria were doing a funny dance with the carpet sweeper. The knife flashed again in the moonlight and then disappeared. Billy let out a loud grunt, and Tater stepped back. Then Billy crumpled to the ground in a heap.

I heard a car pull up and people's voices out in front of the store. The boys heard them, too. They scattered.

"Annie, get over here!" Miss Gloria yelled. I got up as far as my knees. My coat weighed a ton. I squished like wet wash when I moved. Everything shivered, even my teeth.

"Now!" said Miss Gloria. "Hurry! There isn't a minute to lose."

I wriggled out of my coat and lurched over to where Billy lay like a big rag doll on the lawn. Miss Gloria was ripping off pieces of her petticoat.

"Your uncle's hurt real bad. We need to stop the bleeding." Her face scrunched into a frown every time she ripped off another piece. She pointed to just under Billy's left rib. "Put your hand there and apply pressure."

So much blood. My dinner churned in my stomach, but I was too scared to throw up. Miss Gloria quickly stepped out of the rest of her slip and ripped it clean in half.

"He's losing a lot of blood. We got to keep him from spilling any more."

Together, we gently rolled Billy to one side, and she slid the length of slip underneath him. Then we did the same to the other side, and Miss Gloria tied the pieces of slip like a big bandage.

All the while I was thinking that Billy was going to die. I didn't cry 'cause I was so set on keeping him alive. We didn't even hear Grandma and Scooter until they were right next to us.

Grandma let out a cry. "Oh my Lord!" she wailed. "Oh my Lord! Scooter, go call for an ambulance!"

Chapter 17

I tried to crawl right into the ambulance with Billy, but only Grandma was allowed. Besides, she wouldn't hear of me riding along.

If my legs hadn't been full of jelly, I would have stamped my feet and thrown a fit. Billy might die before he got to the hospital, and he'd never know how much I needed him to live. My stomach was in knots, and my teeth chattered. Grandma scarcely looked at me. She wouldn't take her eyes away from Billy.

"I'll see that Annie gets changed out of these wet clothes." Miss Gloria wound her arm around my shoulders and held me close.

"And I'll make sure they get down to the hospital directly," said Scooter. "We'll be right behind you."

The ambulance pulled away from the curb, and its siren screamed into the night. My heart sank.

In the bright light of the kitchen, I got my first look at Miss Gloria's new dress. It was all limp and covered in blobs of red like splashed paint. Back in my room, I pulled off my ruined birthday dress without looking at it. I couldn't get my old jeans on fast enough.

Five minutes later, Miss Gloria and I were in the Buick with Scooter, silently making our way to the hospital. He dropped us off right at the front door and raced off to get his uncle Orville.

We didn't get past the lobby. The sour faced lady at the desk informed us that no children under twelve were allowed to visit in the wards.

"Surely, under these circumstances," said Miss Gloria. But the lady wouldn't budge.

We sat there for the longest time, glum-faced, waiting for news. The nurses scurried around us, their starched uniforms whish-whishing as they passed by. We were still waiting an hour later when Scooter returned with his uncle Orville in tow.

"You look tuckered out," he said. "How's Billy?"

I started to answer but stopped when I saw two policemen coming down the hall with Grandma. They shook her hand, tipped their hats, and walked on by. I noticed Grandma's eyes right away. They were all puffy, and her braid sat lopsided on her head, wisps of hair sticking out all directions. She eased herself into a chair next to me and took a deep breath.

"Billy's going to be fine, but he has a bit of a hospital stay ahead of him." She patted my hand. "Sweetpea, you saved your uncle's life." Grandma's voice had a flutter in it. I figured she was fighting a lump in her throat. She reached for my hand again.

"Miss Gloria knew just what to do, Grandma. I just did what she told me."

Grandma's eyes glistened, and she fished a hanky out of her pocketbook and dabbed at her eyes.

"How can I ever thank you, Gloria? Words aren't enough to tell you what I'm feeling."

Miss Gloria moved over to sit next to Grandma. She linked her arm through Grandma's and took her hand in hers. All at once the whole room had the sniffles. Scooter took out a giant hanky and blew his nose. Grandma looked over at Scooter and muttered something. Scooter leaned closer, but Grandma was already snoring, her chin resting on her chest.

"Your grandma is just plain worn out." Miss Gloria said, fussing with her pocketbook. "We'll let her sleep. You think maybe we can find some ice cream in this place?"

"You go right along," said Scooter. "Uncle Orville and I'll be right here looking out for Hattie. If we hear anything, I'll come find you."

Later, over Dixie cups in the hospital cafeteria, I asked Miss Gloria how she knew what to do for Billy.

"Out in the country, with no doctor or hospital real close — at least one that'd take us folks — well, we had to learn how to take care of ourselves." Miss Gloria studied her ice cream. "There isn't enough in these itty bitty things to feed a bird. How about another one?"

"Why couldn't you go to any old hospital?" I asked when she returned with two more Dixie cups. "Hospitals *have* to take in sick people."

"This time I got you one with orange sherbet and vanilla," she said. "We might just have to eat our way through the cafeteria's ice cream before this night is over."

"Tell me," I said. "Why couldn't you go to any old hospital?"

"Oh, sweet thing." She took her time licking the last of the ice cream off her wooden spoon.

"In the South Negroes can't go everywhere white folks can. It's the law. That's one of the reasons R.J. and I made the decision we'd stay out West after he got out of the army. We were tired of 'White Only' signs and keeping our heads down all the time."

She let out one of those big sighs of hers. "I've said more than I meant to. I must be truly tired." She stood up and reached for my hand, and together we made our way back to the lobby.

Miss Gloria's words were a jumble in my head. Made a person think about a lot of things that didn't seem at all right. I wondered if Grandma knew about what Gloria had told me.

Any conversation with Grandma would have to wait. She was bound and determined to stay the night in Billy's room, and nothing could change her mind. She sent me home but promised that the next morning I'd get to see Uncle Billy. Miss Gloria and I walked out into a cold rain and piled back into the Buick. Scooter dropped off his uncle and told us that he promised Grandma he'd sleep on the cot in the storeroom.

Miss Gloria wouldn't hear of it and made up the Murphy bed for him. I didn't feel much like sleeping in my room, so I went over to Miss Gloria's and got into the other twin bed.

"It's not a night to be in a cold room all by yourself," she said. "We'll have ourselves a slumber party."

It was then I remembered Billy's package. In all the excitement, I'd forgotten all about it.

"I need to go down to the porch and look for something," I said.

"Your medal? I thought about that earlier myself. Then it dropped right out of my head." Miss Gloria grabbed her robe off the bedpost. "C'mon, we'll go down together."

The package was still on the back porch where I'd left it, but we couldn't find the medal.

"I bet it's in the creek," I said.

"We'll look for it tomorrow." Miss Gloria handed me Billy's package. "Go on. Let's see what he gave you."

I untied the string. There, under layers of butcher paper, was a wooden jewel box, polished down to a shine that almost glowed. Right in the middle of the lid was a butterfly carved from three different kinds of wood. It was the most beautiful thing Billy had ever made me. It even had its own tiny lock and key.

"This is the best present ever," I said.

Miss Gloria put her hand on my shoulder. "Indeed! My, I've never seen such fine handiwork. Look at how carefully he's matched the grain. I didn't realize your uncle was such a craftsman. Why, that can be your treasure box."

On our way back upstairs, we had to stop every step or so to examine the butterfly all over again. I'd found the perfect place for my medal, and Miss Gloria agreed that it was the best treasure box in the whole world. We talked a mile a minute to the top of the stairs, and then Miss Gloria stopped in her tracks.

"Listen."

I got quiet real fast. No one was hammering or breaking in, but I heard something. Someone was playing "Amazing Grace" on the harmonica.

"That has to be Scooter," she said. "Why, that boy is full of surprises."

Back in her room, Miss Gloria climbed right into bed and was sound asleep before I had time to say "goodnight." Always made me giggle to hear her snore. She made little puff-puff sounds, not like Grandma's honks and whistles.

I put my treasure box on the side table where I could see it first thing in the morning. I figured I wouldn't be able to sleep a wink, but I got under the covers and started to have me a good long conversation with God.

When I opened my eyes, there was Mr. Truman, standing right at the foot of my bed. In all of the excitement I'd barely had time to give the president a thought, but I was real glad to see him. Before I could say a word, I found myself out by the creek, sitting in the lawn swing. It was snowing outside, but I was warm as toast.

"Sure is something, Sir, the way you can just float around like that. How do you do it?"

"Now, Annie Leigh, that would be giving away state secrets." Mr. Truman took his hat and brushed away bits of snow before sitting down beside me. "Hope I didn't startle you, but after the day Miss Gloria's had, I didn't want to risk waking her. We've got some talking to do."

"Go ahead, Sir. I'm not the least bit sleepy."

"First of all, I want to tell you what a fine speech that was. I almost burst a few buttons, I was so proud. And the way you stepped in to help Billy. Why, I know a few grown men who couldn't have done what you did. Your daddy's coming home to a daughter of exceptional courage."

Mr. Truman's words were real welcome, but it sounded an awful lot like he was making a goodbye speech.

"I know you're just a figurehead of my imagination," I said. "But, that's okay 'cause having our little talks has been just the best."

"It's *figment*, Annie Leigh. A figment of your imagination." His blue eyes twinkled even brighter behind those thick glasses of his. "One thing I know for sure, there's nothing you can't tackle. You come from strong pioneer stock, a long line of fine Howard women."

Mr. Truman pulled out his pocket watch. "I've got to be going, and you have a big day tomorrow."

Well, I wasn't going to miss my last chance. I stepped right up to the President of the United States and gave him a big hug. He gave me one right back. And then, with a tip of his hat and without another word, he was gone.

The next morning I woke up to Miss Gloria shaking my shoulder. Before I could even get my thoughts straight, she was yelling out all sorts of orders like a drill sergeant.

"Get dressed right away and have a little breakfast.

Don't wake Scooter, he's dead to the world. Your grandma called. We need to get down to the hospital. I've ordered us a taxi."

She assured me there was no emergency, but Miss Gloria was dead set on getting to the hospital in record time.

For once, the sourpuss wasn't at the front desk. A lady with big apple cheeks called Grandma to the front, and all three of us went up to Billy's floor.

"Billy's asked for you especially," Grandma said.

Chapter 18

Grandma and Gloria waited in the lobby. I walked to Billy's room, pushed open the door, and peeked in. His face was turned away from me. I didn't notice the little row of stitches on his cheek until I was right next to the bed. His nose was swollen, and both eyes were ringed in black and blue. That big lump was Billy, of course, but all I could think of was movie monsters.

"Hello, twerp," he said. His voice sounded weak and tired.

"Hello, yourself." I swallowed hard to keep my voice from shaking.

"Ma says you saved my life." Billy winced and turned his face away. "Should've saved yourself the trouble."

"What do you mean, saved myself the trouble? And

172

you could say 'thank you.' Besides, it was Gloria who saved your life. Not me." Even all busted up and flat on his back, Billy could be a brat.

"Your Miss Gloria has the answers for everything, don't she." Billy's words came out in little gasps, like it hurt to talk. "She's a marvel, that one."

"Grandma said you wanted to see me. Guess she was wrong."

"Go on, pull up that chair and sit down, kid." Billy tried to ease himself up, but he collapsed back onto the pillows.

"You better not move around too much," I said. "You'll pull out your stitches."

"Aren't you Miss Know-It-All."

"And you look like a Frankenstein monster. All you need, Billy, are pointy teeth and spikes coming out of your head."

"Now, that's no way to treat a fellow when he's down." Billy tried to sound hurt, but I could see he was holding back a smile.

"How come those ol' boys were after you?"

Billy's smile disappeared completely. "Now there you go, pokin' into my business again."

"Billy Howard, I'm not going to fuss with you." The next bed was empty, and I almost crawled under the covers. I wanted nothing more than to sleep.

"Simmer down, Annie Leigh. Ma was right. I got some things to say to you."

"I'm not going to stay if you're just going to be ornery."

"It ain't easy for a fella to admit he's wrong. I'm doing the best I can."

"Sometimes I think you don't care about us, me and Grandma. With Daddy gone and all, you should've been watching out for us instead of causing us more trouble."

"I never was good at doing the right things. It was your dad that did good in school, played baseball, could make anything out of an old block of wood. He knew what he wanted to do with his life from the git-go. Always made Ma proud. Trouble always found me. I didn't have to go look for it."

"You didn't have to take up with those nasty boys and make trouble for Miss Gloria," I said. "And what about the fire? I bet you know a whole lot about that, too." The sound of my voice made me stop short. I had yelled the last part. Here Billy had almost died, and I was yelling at him.

"Hear me out, Annie." Billy's voice had gotten weaker, and his face had gone pale where it wasn't bruised. "You saved my life and . . ."

"*Miss Gloria* saved your life."

"All right, you and Gloria saved my life, and I am beholden to you." Billy went quiet for a moment. "Okay? I never meant harm to come to any of you. Things just got all mixed up after I got out of the army. I don't expect you to understand."

"I understand that you came home from the war all mean and ugly, but you should have been happy just to be back with Grandma and the family. With Daddy missing, I needed you." Fighting back tears took some effort, but I went on. "Mama and Grandma figured Daddy was never coming back, I know they did. But you came back. I knew Daddy would, too."

"But, see, that's the thing. How come I came back without a scratch when my buddies didn't come home at all — and my brother came back without his sight? I was the one who always messed up. I mean, it was your dad taught me carpentry to keep me out of trouble. And I finally found something I was good at. We were going to open us up a business. When he went missing, I just gave up."

"Uncle Billy, you don't need a bit of help with carpentry. Why, that treasure box you made me is the most beautiful present I ever got. I bet you and Daddy can still have a business. He may have lost his sight, but I'm sure he's just as smart as ever."

Billy started to turn away from me, but I saw a funny crooked smile on his face just the same. I went on.

"Grandma says there's lots to do before Daddy gets home. She's going to need a lot of help. Why, she's been running herself ragged. And I'll tell you another thing, I'll never speak to you again if you don't apologize to Miss Gloria for being so mean."

"How'd you get so high and mighty, Missy?"

"You know I'm right." I reached over and touched Billy's face. Suddenly, he looked older than Mr. Teeples. "Does it hurt something fierce?"

"Only when I laugh." But Billy wasn't smiling this time.

We were both quiet for several minutes.

"Remember when I was little?" I said. "You teased the dickens out of me, but you were the one who always patched me up when I scraped my knee or banged up my elbow."

"I'm going to make it up to you, Annie Leigh. I promise." Billy reached for my hand. "How come you didn't just give up on me?"

"First off, you're the only uncle I've got. And I will give up on you if you don't stop feeling sorry for yourself."

It seemed to me that Billy needed a whole lot of patching up. And not just from the knife fight. One day I'd tell him about that morning at the library and how I saw the hurt under all that bullying. Miss Gloria had been right all along. The war had eaten away at him until he was near raw. But there were older hurts, too.

"Would you ask your grandma to step in here?" said Billy. "And your Miss Gloria, too."

"Sure, Uncle Billy. You bet." And I bent over and gave him a big sloppy kiss right on his swollen cheek. He didn't move a muscle.

As I was closing the door, I heard soft sniffling sounds. I'd wait a minute before I found Grandma so Billy wouldn't be caught blubbering. It was the least I could do.

Chapter 19

Uncle Billy came home from the hospital to a house full of crazy people. For days Grandma was cleaning out cupboards and drawers. She had Scooter washing windows and scrubbing everything in sight. I figured any minute she'd ask me to wash down all the canned goods in the store and scrub the potatoes clean.

One morning, Gloria helped me take down all the curtains and give them a good wash. We were outside hanging them up to dry when Scooter came out the back door of the store with a broom and a ladder.

"I'm supposed to clean out the gutters and check the eaves," he said. "Hattie'll have me hanging green leaves on those bare trees any minute now."

Gloria gave me a wink. "Miss Hattie just wants everything perfect when Mr. Eddie and Annie's mama get here."

Scooter just rolled his eyes and headed round to the side of the house.

When Billy saw all the activity going on, he was bound and determined to be part of it.

"I've been meaning to get to those front steps," he said. "They're a disgrace. A fellow could break his neck on all those rough patches."

So right there and then, with one bum arm and his middle wrapped up tight in bandages, he decided nothing would do but to fix those steps. After I helped him find his old tools, I fetched him nails and about a million cups of coffee.

It was cold, but it sure was something watching Billy. He could smooth out a bunch of snags as easy as I could iron a pillowcase. Then I'd sweep up the wood curls, and he'd go on to the next step.

Once in a while he'd give a little jerk. I guessed his arm was giving him trouble or he got a stitch in his side, but he didn't stop until all six steps were smooth as glass and the railing was solid as a rock.

"Now then, we won't have to worry about your daddy breaking his neck," he said.

I believe I was beginning to see the old Billy again.

Mama brought Daddy home the day before Thanksgiving. The taxi pulled up right in front of the house, and we all ran out the door, yelling and waving our arms. Grandma had us wear bright outfits. Turned out Daddy could see shapes and colors.

Miss Gloria had made me a new red velvet dress right out of a picture in *Ladies' Home Journal.* She was dressed in violet, and Grandma wore a new dress, the exact color of the pumpkin pies cooling in the kitchen. Uncle Billy even went out and bought himself a nifty Pendleton shirt.

I was so excited I could hardly speak. Mama got out of the taxi first, and then a tall soldier the color of ebony got out and helped Daddy. At first I just stood there.

"Well, don't be shy," Daddy said, opening up his arms.

I practically threw myself on him. Then Mama pulled us all into one big hug. I let myself be squashed in between them just like we used to do at the town hall dances.

Through the commotion, I heard Miss Gloria let out a big gasp. "My Lord! It's Willie Dupree from Athens!"

When all the yelling and waving died down, we stood around like statues for a second to collect ourselves and get our bearings.

Then Billy reached out and touched Daddy's hand and made like he was going to shake it.

"No deal, little brother," said Daddy. "Nothing will do but a bear hug."

They stood there holding on to each other for quite a while. I looked at Grandma, and she smiled back, her eyes all teary.

Miss Gloria and Willie, the tall dark soldier, stood off in a corner. Catching up on news from home, I figured. Seems Private Dupree was on his way to a new assignment at the army hospital near the air base here in Walla Walla, but first he was to help get Daddy settled.

I didn't want to leave Daddy's side for one minute. I had to keep pinching myself to believe he was really home. We hugged every chance we got. I told Mama all about my speech, and she said when we got home, she'd like to hear it, and she bet Daddy would want to as well.

That reminded me that Gloria and I had never looked

for my medal, and Billy offered to go find it. He made a big deal out of fishing it out of the creek one-handed. Showing off for Daddy.

Miss Gloria cooked us all a Southern meal to celebrate Daddy's homecoming. We had fried chicken and two kinds of potatoes, mashed and sweet. Mr. Dupree seemed mighty pleased with Miss Gloria's candied sweet potatoes, and he did go on about her fine yeast rolls. I was stuffed to the gills. Billy was pretty quiet all through dinner. Grandma nearly fainted when he showed up in the kitchen to help with the dishes.

Later, Grandma told me that Uncle Billy really and truly had tried to make it up to us. I found out why he'd gotten a knife in the ribs. Seems he'd gone to the police with what he knew about the cross burning, and somehow those mean ol' boys found out that he was the one who had squealed on them.

I had always figured Uncle Billy wasn't half so tough as he pretended to be. And if he didn't stop acting like a pill, well, I'd just have to give him a good poke. In my heart, I hoped that maybe a hug every so often would do the trick.

Grandma said we'd sort out all the sleeping arrangements by and by, but she thought it was a fine idea for me to sleep in Miss Gloria's room again for a while. Private Dupree could have the Murphy bed, and Mama and Daddy would sleep in Daddy's old bedroom.

"I can hardly believe that my daddy is just across the hall," I said to Miss Gloria.

We were in her apartment sipping steaming mugs of cocoa. It was late, but I was too excited to sleep. I got up to go stand by the window. Something down by the creek caught my eye. For a minute I thought it might be Mr. Truman in that white suit of his. But it was only snow beginning to pile up in feathery drifts on the swing.

Miss Gloria put down her cup and dabbed her mouth with a hanky.

"And I find it hard to believe that Willie Dupree is down there on that old Murphy bed." She leaned back and closed her eyes. "It's a real blessing how people come into our lives." She sat up and looked at me. "And I do believe that, Annie Leigh. People come into our lives at a particular time for a reason."

And I knew deep in my heart just how true that was.